What People Are Sa

Finally the wait is over and it was worth it! Janet tells another captivating story. She sparked my attention in chapter one, and kept it throughout the book. Alas, I must wait for the next novel.

—Michael Cacciatore, MD OB/GYN

Excellent read. Janet takes complex procedures and breaks them down for everyone's consumption. Highly recommended for both the professional and the novice.

—Roy Edwards, Colonel, United States Army, (Ret.)

I found this book very informative and entertaining. It provides an insightful look at a facet of our military history that has too often been overlooked. The author has a great future ahead that is well deserved.

—Donald L. Finch, Captain, United States Navy, (Ret.)

As a lover of historical and medical fiction, I found it a special treat to find the combination done with such skill. The characters in Shawgo's first novel helped me to remember the true reason why I chose a vocation of healing. These characters also made me proud to be a woman. This second novel does not disappoint and more than re-enforces these sentiments. I challenge you to try to put it down!

—Elizabeth Hutcheson, MD, FACOG

I find Janet's writing style very compelling, leaving the reader to wonder what will be found just around the corner. This is a tribute to all females who sacrifice their lives in the service to others.

—Christine Leblond, Colonel, United States Army, (Ret.)

Wait for Me, catches your attention from the very beginning. Janet has shown the courage of women during a time of war. They answered the call to serve their country and went where the need was greatest.

—Pamela L. Little, Captain, United States Air Force, NC

WAIT FOR ME

WAIT FOR ME

JANET K. SHAWGO

$\mathscr{A}$CKNOWLEDGMENTS

As I was researching information for this book I found many interesting stories from the women who served in the military during World War II. After reading these wonderful stories, I felt cheated. There was no mention of the women who served, or any who were captured or killed during World War II when I was in school. Why were these outstanding women left out of our history for so long? I feel it is important for the reader to know what women accomplished during the war. They made a difference then and continue to make a difference today.

In the article, "Women and World War II: Women in the Military," on *About.com Women's History*, I found the following information:

Women in the Military:
Army 140,000
Navy 100,000
Marines 23,000
Coast Guard 13,000
Air Force (WASP) 1,000
Army and Navy Nurse Corp 74,000

On the same website in, "Women and World War II: Women at Work and Women on the Home Front," there are over six million women listed as having entered the workforce in factories, shipping yards, farms, and anywhere else men held jobs. Housewives had replaced the men who were sent to war, including my mother, who worked in an ammunitions factory. Three million women volunteered for the Red Cross. A total of over sixteen million men and women were involved in World War II.

Blackamericanweb.com includes an article that mentions the "Little-Known Black History Fact: The 6888th Battalion of World War II." This unit was the only all-female African American battalion during World War II and the first to travel overseas. Their unit was called the "six triple eight." These women moved mountains of mail that clogged warehouses. They redirected mail for more than seven million people in the armed service, civilians, and the Red Cross. Their efforts and accomplishments were ignored until 2009. The women of the six triple eight were honored and recognized at the Women's Memorial at Arlington National Cemetery.

From "Nurses in World War II," at Dpsinfo.com, these statistics were found: 201 women died and eighty-three were held prisoners of war by the Japanese for thirty-seven months.

I sometimes forget about the sacrifices made by these men and women. Their love of country and home then and now keep the wolf away from the front door. To those women: You are greatly appreciated, though we may not say it enough.

I wish to give a special thank you to the veterans at the bingo hall who shared their stories with me. There is no history like that which sits in front of you recalling the smallest details. Some of the conversations we had were painful. There were tears and choked words of friends and comrades lost so many years ago. Many of the men I talked with were decorated heroes with purple hearts and silver and bronze stars. One man told me, "I am no hero; the real heroes are the ones who never came home."

I want to thank the staff at the Lone Star Museum in Galveston, Texas. They were kind enough to educate me on the Texan and the B-17. These planes are in working order and still fly today there at the museum.

To my sister, Joan, friend, Pat, nieces and nephews who encouraged me through these books. I love and appreciate you. Jackie, my travel friend, thanks for the French lessons and your assistance with the proper usage of phrases. To my readers, thank you for your kind words and support.

My continuing appreciation to my publisher, Two Harbors Press. Your staff makes me feel like family.

✐EDICATION

This book is dedicated to the women and men in our armed services—past, present, and future.

To my family who served and died in World War II, including two who are forever entombed on the USS Arizona.

May we always remember those who paid the ultimate price for our way of life.

$\mathscr{P}$ROLOGUE

December 7, 1941
Pearl Harbor, Hawaii

MAKESHIFT HOSPITAL INSIDE THE HOME OF A GENERAL

I can't see. Why can't I see? Is anyone there? Can someone help me? I keep asking but no one seems to hear me. The last thing I remember was going to mess for breakfast with Digger and Bender. Digger, Bender, where are you guys? Why won't someone answer me? Where am I? Pain. God, please let someone see me.

I feel a hand touch me, soft words mumbling. I can barely hear. Why can't I hear?! I feel my face being wiped off and something touching the side of my head. Someone is wrapping a bandage around my eyes. My hands are shaking as I reach and feel the hands that are attending to my injury. They are small—a woman's hands—and the scent of lilacs. She smells like the spring blossoms after a rain. Her hands finish their work, a pat on my shoulder, and then she is gone.

It seems like forever but I begin to hear more mumbling. A man's voice tells me that my eyes have been burned and he will have the nurse rewrap them. The doctor says whoever bandaged them did a fine job, looks like a field dressing. When he asks me if I remember what happened I try to speak but just shake my head no. The soothing voice of a woman tells me Pearl has been attacked by Japan; that I was injured and brought to a makeshift hospital in the general's home. I point to my ears and she says my eardrums maybe ruptured. I may have a problem hearing for a while. She says she must leave but will return with pain medication. I guess there are several nurses here.

I begin to hear moaning, screaming, and then cursing. The voice of the doctor who had talked to me is telling someone named Larry to move on and help the living. He tells Larry the dead belong to God now. I can hear this man saying he will not let others forget what happened here today. He swears on the bodies of the men in this room that America will know of their sacrifice. He will write stories for all to read and he will tell of the need for doctors and nurses in

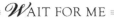

the months ahead. This man says he will ask for those with medical experience to join the service.

I then feel a hand on my shoulder and a familiar voice. Digger tells me he and Bender made it. They both have some cuts and burns but they are okay. They congratulate me and tell me I am going home, no fighting for me. I motion for a cigarette. Both laugh, telling me my throat was burned.

The nurse returns and tells me she has something for the pain. As I begin to drift off to sleep I hear Digger and Bender talking about the oddly dressed woman helping the wounded inside. Bender says she looks out of place in that long blue checkered dress.

CHAPTER ONE

September 23, 1940
New York
Jefferson/Shaw Residence

*J*ean Anne White-Shaw was reading the newspaper, listening to Glenn Miller on the radio and waiting for her son to come downstairs. He was to join her for lunch before her meeting this afternoon and she did not wish to be late. Jean had organized a group of women to help the less fortunate. The White and Shaw families had prospered during what many had called desperate times. During the First World War, so many poor souls in the South throughout the dust bowl and the depression were left without food, shelter, or clothing. Jean, at fifty years old, intended to make sure her daughter did not become insensitive to the needs of others, as teenagers sometimes do. Beatrice would be the last of her children left at home, now that Lawrence was leaving. She tired of the arguments each night between Jefferson and Lawrence. Jean could not understand how a father and son were unable to have a simple conversation without harsh words. Lawrence was a man, and his decision to leave New York was his alone. Lawrence's footsteps on the stairs ended Jean's thoughts for the moment.

"Good afternoon, Mother," Larry said as he leaned down and kissed his mother's cheek.

Jean looked at her son, who was dressed in a pair of black slacks and a green shirt that matched his eyes. She stood and followed him to the buffet. "Lawrence, I don't understand why you feel the need to go to Hawaii. You have a future here—a legacy—and your grandfather needs you."

"Mother, you know why I am leaving. And would you please call me Larry? Lawrence is such a formal name reserved for someone I'm not," Larry answered. "More coffee?"

Jean shook her head no.

"Mother, this job is a wonderful opportunity for me. My New York education is the best Father could buy. I am great at what I do; just read my stories." He smiled at her. "You know how much it took for me to get this job. I need to be on my own, away from Father. He is driving me crazy. Emmitt is fine running Grandfather's business. I really want to do this. I am tired of the New York winters. I want to live somewhere warm."

"I am just concerned about the unrest overseas; all this talk of America involving itself in another war. Your grandfather's health is not good; think of him," Jean responded.

"Mother, please stop with the guilt. I have to go. Grandfather will understand."

"What about Arlene?"

"What do you mean?" Lawrence asked.

"I thought the two of you . . . " Jean began but was cut off by her son.

"There is no two of us, Mother. Arlene is fun, but that's all, end of story," Lawrence said.

"Does she know that?" Jean asked.

"She's planning a Halloween party for my birthday next month. She'll figure it out when I don't show up," Lawrence answered.

"Do you think that's fair?" Jean continued.

"About as fair as she was when I saw Milford Hillman III leaving her house at one in the morning."

Jean paused for a moment, a little embarrassed that she'd asked one too many questions of her son. She decided to move the conversation away from Arlene. "I want you to go see your grandfather before you leave."

"Why?"

"He has something to give you."

"Do you know what it is?" he asked.

"I am not sure," Jean answered.

"It must be important or he wouldn't have mentioned it to you."

*P*hillip Alfred White sat behind his desk at the *White Daily Journal* looking at the last story about to go to print. The radio was playing "What's New" by Bing Crosby. Phillip had rarely missed a day of work except for the birth of his children. He knew the time would come very soon when he would not be able to work as he had all these years. Phillip had hoped that Lawrence would take over the newspaper, but his life was headed down another path. Emmitt, his oldest grandson, would continue the family business and the finances. Lawrence had a spark, always in the right place at the right time to get the story. His specialty was to obtain the unobtainable, and that ability made the job in Hawaii a completed deal. Lawrence was like Samuel, the older brother Phillip never knew except through written word and stories from his mother. His father, Eric, refused to talk about Samuel to anyone except Mother and Franklin Prichard.

Phillip first noticed similarities between Lawrence and Samuel's writings after reading old news stories. Writing styles so close that at times he felt as though he was reading from only one author. Phillip reached over to open the safe—an antique, Emmitt kept reminding him. It contained all things of importance to him, such as the deed to the *Franklin Weekly*, now the *White Daily Journal*. There were Samuel's last handwritten notes from Gettysburg. Phillip then took out the first edition of *The Women Who Travel in War*, by Eric Samuel White, Jr., and Franklin Alfred Prichard. He carefully removed his mother's Bible and placed it in front of him. In the Bible was an envelope that contained two items he needed to give to Lawrence. He opened the envelope and took out the necklace and note that were in Samuel's possession when his body was brought back from Gettysburg. Phillip looked at the necklace; black velvet ribbon and a simple silver heart setting with a pink stone. He turned it over and looked at the initials on the back: SJB; he gently held a note with three words on it: *I promise. Sarah.* Neither Phillip nor any member of his family knew the meaning of the words left in the pocket of a dead man. The only thing he was sure of was that these two items belonged with Lawrence.

CHAPTER TWO

Phillip looked out his office window and saw his tall, hand-some, twenty-seven-year-old grandson walk through the front door. Lawrence was properly attired for a business day in New York, gray double-breasted suit and a fedora. Lawrence, or Larry—as he insisted we call him now—had the typical all-American build: tall at 6'3" and brown hair with a hint of red. His stunning trait was his unusual green eyes, eyes that no one ever forgot once they met him. Phillip remembered his mother telling him Samuel had green eyes. She called them haunting.

"Good morning, Grandfather." Larry was cheerful and smiled.

"Morning was about three hours ago, Lawr . . . Larry," Phillip tried to be stern.

"Mother said you have something to give me."

"I do. Can you spare a few minutes out of your busy schedule to take me to the coffee shop down the street?" Phillip asked.

"Sir, it would be my pleasure to buy you a cup of joe," Larry said.

Phillip stood and took his hat and jacket off a hook. "Fools Rush In," by Glenn Miller, was playing as they started to leave. They headed for the main door when both men heard a familiar voice.

"Lawrence! Lawrence! Where are you taking Grandfather?" Emmitt blocked their exit.

"Larry is taking me to the drug store to get my medicine," Phillip answered and hoped that Larry would go along with his story.

"I will send someone for your medicine," Emmitt responded.

"Damn it, man! I need some fresh air. I have a right to come and go as I please," Phillip said, his voice grew louder.

"Okay, but stay away from the coffee shop and those greasy donuts. You know what the doctor said about your heart," Emmitt said and looked at his brother. "Lawrence, I am counting on you to be the adult here."

"To the drug store and back," Larry said, and then turned and smiled at his grandfather.

"Yeah, yeah, I know coffee is bad and greasy donuts aren't good for my heart. Old bastard doesn't know crap," Phillip said.

Larry laughed as they left the building.

*H*elen's Corner Coffee Shop

Phillip loved this coffee shop with its bright-colored seats at the counter. His favorite was a corner booth with red seats and a yellow table. The smell of fresh brewed coffee and frying donuts met Larry and Phillip as they walked inside. Before Phillip could take his hat off a loud female voice was heard from behind the counter.

"PW!" a woman called and quickly headed toward the two men.

"Helen!" Phillip reached out and hugged a rather large woman in a white uniform and starched headband with HELEN'S written on it. She had red lips and heavy black eyeliner, and proceeded to talk and chew gum at that same time.

"Honey, where the hell have you been?" Helen asked Phillip. "And who is this handsome young man?" Her smile grew bigger.

"I am being held captive by Emmitt and that bastard doctor of mine. This young man arranged my escape. Larry Shaw, meet Helen Hanaby. Larry is my grandson," Phillip said as both men took off their hats.

"Sugar, it's nice ta meet ya. What can I get you two?" Helen asked.

"My regular, if you please," Phillip said.

"I will have the same," Larry told Helen. "And it's White, Larry White."

Phillip smiled.

Helen's eyes widened. "I know who you are. Your articles are wonderful. Is it true you are going to Honolulu to work? Tell me it ain't so, honey," she asked.

"I am afraid the rumors are correct. I will be leaving New York very soon," Larry said.

"Sugar, we are going to miss you and those good stories," Helen said as she turned and walked away.

"Larry, we need to sit back here away from the window just in case your brother didn't believe me," Phillip said and pointed to a back corner booth.

Helen returned with two cups of coffee and four donuts, two chocolate-covered and two cream-filled covered in chocolate. "Here you go. I'll be back to warm you up later," Helen told them, winked, and walked off to serve the long line waiting.

Larry looked at his grandfather. "No wonder Emmitt questioned us before we got away, Grandfather," Larry said and picked up his coffee cup.

"Your brother is too damn nosey for his own good. I am too old to care at this point in my life. When I die I want to die happy and with a donut in my hand," Phillip told him. "Your grandmother would have understood. God rest her soul."

"I'll put that on your tombstone then," Larry said and picked up a donut.

An hour later, after three cups of coffee and one more donut each, Phillip was ready to talk to Larry. He hoped his grandson would listen and not put him in a straight jacket.

"Larry, meet me outside. I want to go for a walk," Phillip told him.

Phillip watched Larry grab his hat and walk outside to wait for him. He made a stop at the restroom, paid his bill, and left a nice tip for Helen.

"Don't stay away so long, honey." Helen kissed Phillip on the cheek and handed him a small sack of his favorites.

Phillip walked outside, put his fedora on, and looked at his grandson. "There's a park at the end of the block and I need some sun. Let's walk."

Larry was happy to be with his grandfather, but all the stalling had made him suspicious and a little nervous. He lit a cigarette as they walked down the street. They found a quiet place and a bench to sit on.

"Lawrence, Larry, I have something that I need to give you before you leave for Hawaii. I am very proud of you and a little sad you are going so far away. I know you have a path you feel you need to take and no one else can choose it for you," Phillip said, and then took an envelope out of his coat pocket and handed it to Larry.

Larry opened the envelope and almost dropped the necklace and note that fell into his hand. He looked at his grandfather.

"These were in your great uncle's possession when his body was brought back from Gettysburg. The story my mother told me was that Samuel fell in love with a Confederate nurse. He was writing stories about the nurses and was traveling with them. They became separated; the reason unknown, but Samuel found her at Gettysburg. He was injured in an explosion and died in her arms. This nurse's name was Sarah Bowen. The Bowens and Whites had been connected in some type of friendship years before marriages and children. We had records at one time due to a trust set up with your great uncle's money, but there was a fire at the bank and all records were lost. I understand she was from a small town south of Augusta, Georgia, where her family farmed. It's funny, with interest the trust is still increasing for her heirs. The money reverted back to our family. It was safe even with the bank failures during the depression," Phillip stopped for a moment.

Larry was trying to be patient; he knew this story was important to his grandfather. He would give his grandfather the time needed and listen.

"Your uncle Matthew was a war correspondent in World War I. He took the necklace with him without my knowledge when he left for war. Matthew told me later he felt it would be a good luck charm. When your uncle returned from the war he brought the necklace back to me. He said, *Dad, you need to keep this.* Then he told me his story. "Matthew and a troop of men were pinned down in a trench by gunfire, thought it was the end for all of them. When it seemed all was lost and the men were praying, he looked out across the field and saw a woman. She motioned for him to follow. Matthew alerted the sergeant and the men. They followed him; no one was injured or killed." Phillip stopped.

"A woman on a battlefield? Who was she?" Larry asked.

"Let me finish before you ask any questions. Once they were all safe he began to search for her, but no one was there. Matthew never said a word to anyone in the company, as no one had seen her except him. He described her to me when he brought the necklace back—blonde hair, about 5' 5", couldn't see her eyes but she was wearing a blue checkered dress with blood on it. Matthew said he could smell lilacs in the dead of winter." Phillip finished.

"You're not telling me that woman is the same woman your brother went back to find, are you?" Larry's expression was one of concern for his seventy-seven-year-old grandfather.

"All I am telling you is what your uncle told me. You can believe it or not," Phillip told him.

Larry thought his uncle had been mistaken; it was probably another soldier who had led them out of danger. Matthew had died just a year ago, so there was no way to go talk with him about what really happened on the battlefield.

"Grandfather, why are you giving these to me?" Larry asked.

"These belong to you now," Phillip said.

Larry loved his grandfather and took them to please this man. Phillip was the reason he had became a reporter.

"Thank you, I will keep them in a safe place," Larry said.

"No! I want you to keep them with you when you travel always, promise me," Phillip was adamant.

Larry looked surprised at this last statement. "Of course. I promise, always."

"Good, now take me back to the prison. Your brother will be pulling what's left of his hair out."

Larry and Phillip walked back to the newspaper. When Phillip had hung his coat and hat up, he turned, hugged his grandson, and patted him on the back.

"Take care of yourself, Larry, and keep your word," Phillip warned.

"A White always keeps his word, Grandfather," Larry said.

"Now get out of here and send me a postcard from Hawaii."

Larry was headed out of the *Journal*, but first stopped and turned to look back at his grandfather one more time. He could see him pat the center of his chest.

I guess he shouldn't have had that extra donut, Larry said to himself.

CHAPTER THREE

October 1, 1940
Leland, Mississippi
John's Crop Dusting Service

*B*utch Johns stood outside the hangar in his overalls and plaid shirt looking at the sky. He could hear his brother inside working on one of the planes. The conversation between man and machine was not a good one. When he didn't see or hear anything from above, he went inside.

"Lewis! Lewis! Where the hell is the Piper?" Butch asked.

"Dealer has it, Butch," Lewis answered his brother.

"Damn, I should have known," Butch told him.

"Dealer was here at daybreak working on the Pitcairn, changed the oil in the Waco and said it was time to fly. The next time I looked up the Piper was gone," Lewis said.

"I guess Dealer will come back when it's time to eat," Butch said and walked off. He now had to figure out how to keep his planes in the air so the bank wouldn't take them.

*D*ealer Johns circled for the last time before bringing in the Piper after an hour of flying. The sunshine and fresh air was something she had always enjoyed since learning to fly alone three years ago. Paw said, *I was born to fly.* Dealer banked and brought the plane in with a perfect landing. The plane taxied to the hangar where Dealer could see Butch. There must be something important to discuss but it would have to wait until the motor died and the propeller stopped.

Dealer took off the safety belt and crawled out of the plane, adjusted her leather jacket and scarf, placed wood blocks under the wheels, and ran an ungloved hand across the plane.

"Dealer! Where the hell have you been? There's work to do or there won't be anything left for you to fly. We have to figure something else to do to bring in money," Butch rambled on.

Dealer took off the cap and let her long, red curly hair fall to her shoulders. She wrinkled her freckled nose and said, "Well, we can't let that happen, can we?"

Dealer put her arm around her paw's big arm and they walked back to the hangar.

"Is the radio on?" Dealer asked.

"Yes, and on the station for that silly Buck Rogers and the twenty-fifth century," Butch told her.

"A girl can dream, can't she, Paw?"

Dealer watched her father just shake his head.

*B*utch looked at his daughter as she took off her jacket and turned up the radio. Deelyn Ernest Johns was the oldest of his and Jinny's six children. When Jinny told him she was pregnant he just knew it would be a boy. They were so sure that Jinny promised her paw their child would carry his name. Deelyn was a surprise but carried his name as promised.

"Paw, come listen. I love this program," Dealer told him.

"In a minute."

Butch remembered the way she got the nickname. Lewis gave it to her as a child. She was always wheeling and dealing, getting what she wanted, from plane rides to candy. She really earned it by getting dusting jobs for the business over the last two years. Dealer loved playing poker, one more thing she was good at in addition to being a dang good mechanic. Butch counted on his daughter, who would turn twenty on the thirteenth of this month, as if she were a man. Something he would regret in the months to come.

CHAPTER FOUR

1940
Halloween Night

$\mathcal{L}$arry closed his suitcase and laid out his travel clothes for his long plane ride the next day. The radio was turned down but he could hear "When You Wish Upon a Star" being sung by Bing Crosby. He would have to make at least one, maybe two, overnight stops before he arrived in Honolulu. The newspaper was more than kind to extend his start date so that he could stay for his grandfather's funeral.

Phillip Alfred White died in his sleep two days prior due to a massive heart attack, according to his physician. Larry smiled and wondered if there had been a donut and a cup of coffee on the nightstand next to his bed. He was buried earlier in the day in the family plot next to his wife, son Matthew, Eric, Julia, and Samuel.

The knock on his door would be his mother. Larry knew she had come to say goodbye.

"Lawrence, may I come in?" Jean asked.

Larry opened the door; his mother, still in her black suit from the funeral, walked in and sat down on his bed.

"Has everyone left?" Larry asked.

"Yes. I see you have finished packing," Jean said.

"The rest was shipped weeks ago. My flight is at 6:00 a.m. I will have to be there early. Are you coming with Father and me to the airport?" Larry asked out of courtesy.

"No, I am going to stay here. I have lost enough for one day," Jean told him. "Arlene came by this evening asking for you."

"I know. I appreciated you telling her I was not taking any company at this time, Mother."

"Lawrence, you need to talk to her at some point and explain your avoidance. Call her now or once you arrive in Honolulu. She deserves to know why you have stopped the relationship," Jean said.

"Maybe, but now is not the time," Larry answered. "A dear Arlene letter might be appropriate."

Larry knew his mother's stern look meant she did not approve of his last statement.

"You have a long trip ahead of you, so I will say goodnight." Jean stood to leave. She hugged and kissed her son. "I want you to call when you get settled."

"I will."

"Will you return for the reading of Dad's will?" Jean asked.

"No," Larry began. "Grandfather gave me what had been most important to him before he died."

The radio was playing "And the Angels Sing," by Bing Crosby.

CHAPTER FIVE

November 21, 1940
Augusta, Georgia
Thanksgiving

*S*usan Jane Bowen had about two hours left on the train before it would arrive in Augusta. She was happy to be going home for Thanksgiving. Due to the jobs she had taken over the last few months caring for elderly women who traveled and needed a nurse, which paid very well, she had saved enough money to stay home for a few months. Susan had gone to nursing school in Savannah right out of high school. After she graduated she worked in the hospital there for a year. She saved money and began to look for jobs outside of Georgia. The newspaper classified section had jobs for private duty nurses with the chance to travel. Susan had considered applying to be a stewardess with the airlines, as they were required to also be nurses. Travel was all she talked about in nursing school. She remembered the other students calling her a gypsy.

Susan was in California in 1939, working in a clinic, when she read about the earthquake in Chile. There was a call for volunteers, doctors, and nurses. She contacted the number in the paper and went with other medical volunteers to help. Susan opened her purse to look for the bottle of lavender. She applied a small amount to the base of her neck for the headache that was beginning. When she returned the bottle to its place the edge of a picture in the side pocket of her purse could be seen. Susan took it out. There were two women with arms around each other smiling despite the dust, dirt, and devastation of the Chilean earthquake.

Susan remembered the day she met Judy Lowe, her roommate in South America. She was being led to a tent where she could hear someone singing "The Old Rugged Cross." Susan stopped as tears formed in the corners of her eyes. Her mother had sung in the church choir and that was her favorite song. The moment they met a special bond had begun between them. When Susan left she promised Judy she would write and keep in touch. Judy had worked so hard to become a good nurse, breaking away from the stereotype most women were expected to be in the 1930s. Susan recalled their last conversation about the names Judy had been called over the last few years—black, colored, African; many Susan refused to think about. Judy said she preferred Susan's name above all . . . friend. She would send a letter once she settled and unpacked. Susan's love of home and family had brought her back, plus the last letter from Angie. Her cousin asked her to come home for a few weeks to help with family business; that was all it said. She was anxious to see Aunt Sarah's school, replenish her stock of herbs, and help prepare the fall plants for storage. Susan had been taught at an early age how to heal with nature; now a nurse, she felt both could be used in harmony.

Susan looked up as the train pulled into the Augusta station. She stepped off the train, with the help of the conductor, in her black travel suit. She looked back to make sure the seams were straight on her nylons. Susan's strawberry blonde hair lay on her shoulders in a slight wave. The weather was nice in Augusta today. The headache that started a few hours ago was gone thanks to the lavender oil.

"Susan, Susan, over here!"Angie Marie called to her cousin. She ran and almost knocked Susan over. "It's so good to have you home. We need you here so bad. Please say you will stay here for a while! Please."

Susan looked at her twenty-two-year-old cousin. She had remained petite compared to Susan's 5'7". Angie wore a striped pair of grey slacks and a pullover sweater that complimented her hazel eyes. Susan and Angie had grown up together with their families living close and farming together. They were like sisters, though Susan was three years older. Susan took her hand and pushed the curly auburn hair out of her cousin's eyes.

"Angie, does Grammie Deanna know you are wearing pants in public?" Susan asked, and then laughed.

"No, and don't you tell her either! I snuck away. Where is your luggage?" Angie asked. "I brought Jerry and Eugene Long to help. I figured you would have several pieces."

"Oh, please tell me you didn't bring them," Susan tried not to get mad. "I can't stand Eugene. You know that, Angie."

"I know, but Jerry and I have been going out dancing on the weekends when I'm not working at the hospital, and its Eugene's car," Angie answered.

"I see you passed your tests. Congratulations! Another nurse in the Bowen family . . . the tradition continues," Susan said. "How is Aunt Sarah's school doing?"

"That's the other thing we need to talk about, but not right now," Angie answered quickly.

Susan was upset that there might be a problem with the school. Sarah's school was a family legacy. It bode well to her life and what Sarah did for the community after the Civil War. A legacy Susan intended to see continue.

Angie and Jerry found Susan's luggage and all three waited for Eugene to pull his 1938 Ford station wagon to the front of the building.

"Susan, what's buzzin', cousin?" Eugene asked as he walked up and tried to hug Susan.

Susan stepped back, almost falling to avoid his embrace. "I'm fine, Eugene, thank you."

Susan had not forgotten how Eugene would chase her and Angie home from school. He thought throwing dead frogs, small garden snakes, rotted fruit, or whatever was available to upset them was funny. Once they grew up and were old enough to fight back he stopped. Eugene was a good mechanic at the auto shop in Waynesboro, but Susan's only intention at this point was to get home. Jerry, the younger brother, was handsome and wanted to make something of his life. He worked at the shop with Eugene but had saved enough money to go to college next fall. Once everyone had a seat in the wagon the questions came about Susan's travel, along with Angie's updates on family and friends in the community. The radio was playing "Beat Me Daddy, Eight to the Bar," by the Andrew Sisters, as they headed to the main road home.

"Susan, how can you just work for a short time and move on?"

Eugene asked.

"Easy, I don't look back once I leave. It's on to the next job, next city, and new experience," Susan answered.

"Well, I want to stay home and close to family,"Angie said.

"What about you, Jerry? What do you want to do?" Susan asked him.

"I want to go to school and become a teacher. Maybe stay in Waynesboro or go to Atlanta. I hear the money is good for teachers and nurses." He looked at Angie.

"Did you open the house?" Susan inquired.

"Not the big house, your mom's. Is that all right?" Angie asked.

"Yes, I am not ready to go up to the big house just yet," Susan said.

"Mother and Dad will be happy to see you, and of course Gramps and Grammie, too," Angie told Susan.

"How are they doing?" Susan asked.

"Mom and Dad are fine. Gramps and Grammie, well, they're old, and each time one of them gets sick we worry it will be the last time," Angie said.

"Are they living at your house now?" Susan asked.

"Yes, and they talk about Sarah, James, and Martha with such detail; but they can barely remember what they ate for breakfast."

"We all get old, Angie," Susan said.

"I know. I just don't want to watch them die. Oh, Susan, I'm sorry," Angie said quickly.

"It's okay, Angie."

The rest of the ride to Waynesboro was quiet.

Once they arrived it was obvious that the call for a family gathering had been given. She knew there would be food, drink, and talk until late at night. Susan was barely in the front door when she was bombarded with hugs, kisses, and pats on the back. She made the gauntlet to the stairs and to Angie's room, where she would stay for the next few days. She changed clothes and put on a pair of black slacks she bought in California and a red pullover sweater and flats. There were some things that didn't change, and as long as she could remember, Grandmother Martha had worn pants. This was another Bowen tradition that carried on even today. Susan returned downstairs, where she saw Angie and Jerry having a quiet conversation in the corner of the room.

"Jerry, where is Eugene?" Angie asked.

"He went to start the car; we have to get home. Can you walk me to the car?" Jerry asked.

"Susan, could you tell Mother I will be back in a minute?" Angie asked.

"Is that all you need?" Susan said, and smiled as she watched Angie take Jerry's hand and walk out the front door.

Susan had forgotten what it was like to be home. When Angie returned inside Uncle Henry called for the blessing before the meal and then the onslaught began. Susan could not remember the last home-cooked meal she had eaten. Uncle Henry and the boys played music the rest of the afternoon and into the night. The Bowens sang, danced, and laughed until the old folks needed to go to bed. I remembered that I was not a guest and headed into the kitchen to help Angie with the dishes, but Aunt Ida ran me out.

Susan was still worried about their great aunt's school but too tired to talk to Angie about it tonight. She walked by the family room to tell everyone goodnight and was once again met with family greetings welcoming her back home. Aunt Ida met her at the stairs with a cup of chamomile tea.

"I thought you might want this," Ida said.

"You know me all too well," Susan answered.

The stairs were familiar with fond memories of chasing cousins up and down them, but tonight it had become almost a chore to get to the top step. Susan opened her overnight case and searched for a nightgown. She found the photos of the people she loved, including Great-Aunt Sarah. Susan had been told she had the same blue eyes as her great-aunt. Susan would never leave Waynesboro without the items that meant so much to her. She finished her nightly hygiene cares and cup of tea, and then crawled under fresh sheets and warm quilts and fell asleep with no dreams or nightmares. It was good to be home.

8:00 a.m., November 22, 1940

*D*r. William Benjamin drove his 1938 Black Buick Special up to Henry and Ida Bowens' home. He had been searching for property to open an office for the last few months. Folks in

town told him a few days earlier about an empty building that had
been a school teaching the art of healing, but it had been closed for
some time. Bill needed an office and he wanted a calmer life after
working in Savannah. He needed to get back to his roots, and this
was the place to start. He knew it was early but he would like to get
started on a proposal for the property should the owners be agree-
able. He hoped to work out a reasonable deal and get to the bank
in the next few days. Once Bill stopped and got out of his car he
stretched his six-foot frame and became aware of the smell and feel
of the Georgia autumn. He left his suit and necktie at the boarding
house and hoped these people were accustomed to casual. He heard
laughter and could smell coffee as he walked up the stairs to the
front porch.

"*A*ngie, will you go see if Susan is ready for breakfast?" Ida
asked her daughter.

Angie ran upstairs and opened the door to her bedroom and
found Susan up and dressed.

"Well, I am glad to see you still remember how to get up in the
morning," Angie told her cousin.

Susan turned around grabbed a pillow and threw it at her.

"Mom said come to breakfast," Angie said.

"I am on my way; need to fix my hair first," Susan answered.

"Mom is setting the table," Angie said. She watched Susan pin
back her hair where the natural wave ran across the top and put a
quick wipe of mascara on her lashes. Susan was dressed in the same
black slacks but wore a green sweater this morning.

"Angie, I want to walk down to the corner and check the school.
Then we can talk about what has happened since I've been gone."

Angie did not reply as they headed for the stairs.

Ida heard both women coming downstairs. She had been up
early feeding the chickens, collecting eggs, and making breakfast.
Just another day. There was a knock on the front door as Susan
walked past.

"Good Lord, who could that be this time of morning?" Ida asked.

"Susan, can you answer the door? I need to get these biscuits out before they burn."

Susan stopped and opened the door. She could not believe who was standing on the porch.

"Hello," Bill began.

"Dr. Benjamin, is that you?" Susan asked.

"Susan Bowen, what are you doing here?" Bill returned the question.

"My family lives here," Susan answered. "Come in, please."

Ida looked up to see Susan and a stranger walk into the dining room, where the rest of the family was seated.

"Aunt Ida, Uncle Henry, this is Dr. William Benjamin from Savannah. I met him at the hospital after I graduated from nursing school," Susan told her family.

Ida watched as Susan looked at this man who stood in her home. His black hair was neatly cut and his brown eyes had a spark to them. Ida thought his weight was a little thin for his height. This doctor was a very handsome man, too.

"And the hospital was never the same after you left. You are a good nurse, Susan," Bill told everyone.

Uncle Henry stood and shook his hand. "Son, I don't know what your business is but we never start anything on an empty stomach; have a seat and break bread with us."

"Susan, set another place," Ida said.

"No, I don't want to intrude," Bill began.

"Nonsense, there is plenty and you look like you could use a good home-cooked meal to me," Ida told him.

"Aunt Ida!" Susan was shocked.

Bill laughed. "Does it really show that bad?"

"I am afraid so, son," Henry said.

"Well, guess I better eat then," Bill told him as he sat down next to Susan.

Hands were joined, grace said; Ida watched Bill eat as though he had been starved for days.

*S*usan and Angie cleared the table. She hadn't thought about Dr. Benjamin since she had left the hospital. He had been a good friend to the nurses. His kindness and willingness to teach made him a target by others who felt nurses weren't capable of learning. The coffee pot finished perking and Susan took it to the table.

"Dr. Benjamin, what brings you out to our home today?" Henry asked.

"I am looking for a place to open my practice. I was told by the town folk that the empty building at the end of the road might be for sale," Bill began.

"Empty, for sale, what are you talking about?" Susan looked at Angie and her aunt.

"Well, Doc, I will leave you with the women. They are the ones you will have to talk to. I don't have any say on that property or what happens to it. It's been a pleasure; and if you survive the next few minutes I hope you'll come back again," Henry stood and shook his hand again. "Josh, Jacob, time to go."

Angie's two brothers left with their father. There was always work to do, even if it had been Thanksgiving the day before.

"Susan, since you have been gone things have not gone well. The trust money kept the school up until it stopped coming. Our school fund had been shared as it was meant to be, and we just couldn't make it stretch anymore. I'm sorry. I know the school means a lot to all of us, but we just couldn't keep it open," Ida told Susan.

Ida watched the disbelief in Susan's eyes. She knew Susan loved the school and thought, along with the rest of the family, that this would never happen. Ida's memories rushed back, remembering all the knowledge Susan and Angie had obtained in the school. The knowledge they both had when it came to nature and its healing abilities were taught in the school. She now knew Susan felt like she had let her great aunt down. Ida watched as the tears spilled over and ran down her niece's face.

"Susan, would you consider selling or renting the building to me?" Bill asked.

"I don't want to sell it," Susan answered.

"Then let me rent the school? The community is aware of the location, which will be good for me. If you will let me go inside and look, maybe we can reopen a section of it for the school. This will allow your family to continue the classes of healing with nature," Bill told them.

They all looked at him.

"I did my homework on the school and what was taught there. I feel there's room for both as long as it doesn't interfere with more serious conditions," Bill told them.

"Dr. Benjamin, what happened in Savannah?" Susan asked.

"I'm not really sure, but one morning I realized there was something missing. I wanted to spend time with my patients instead of running in for a few minutes and then leaving them alone with more questions than answers. I became tired of not allowing my patients to have a choice and not being allowed to educate them," Bill answered.

"Susan, let's talk about the options Dr. Benjamin is offering. This could be the answer to my nightly prayers," Ida said.

Susan looked at Bill. "I need some time."

"I understand. I'm at Miss Mayes' boarding house in town," Bill responded.

"Mary Mayes?" Ida asked him.

"Yes."

"Young man, you go back there and get your things right now. We have plenty of room out here and I won't charge you a thing. Mary Mayes is charging you four times what anyone else in town would charge, old bat! You get back out here today," Ida's tone was angry.

"I don't want to impose. I may be here a while looking for other property if we cannot come to an agreement," Bill explained.

"It doesn't matter. We have homes not being used and you will have all the privacy you need," Ida said.

"Would this evening be appropriate?" Bill asked.

"I'll go open gramps and grammie's home," Angie spoke up.

"Then it's done; dinner will be at six," Ida announced.

"Susan, I know this has been a shock for you. I would appreciate it if you would consider my offer. We can all go to the school and walk through together," Bill told her.

"That will be fine, Dr. Benjamin," Susan answered.

"Susan, please drop the doctor and call me Bill. We aren't in the clinical setting anymore and it would make me feel more at ease considering the situation."

"I will let you know something in the next few days," Susan told him.

"Mrs. Bowen, I want to thank you for breakfast. I look forward to dinner," Bill told Ida.

"Angie will open the house and I will get fresh linens up there this afternoon," Ida responded.

"I will be happy to pay you what I am paying Miss Mayes," Bill told her.

"I'm not concerned about the money," Ida said.

Bill stood and headed toward the front door. The women followed, walking him out to his car. They stood and watched as he drove away.

Susan turned to Angie and her aunt once the car was out of sight. "What the hell happened while I was gone? That money should have lasted for generations of Bowens."

"I didn't want to air our dirty laundry in front of a stranger, Susan Jane. If you come back inside I will tell you what really happened to the money," Ida said. "And don't curse. You remind me of your grandmother Martha when you do that!"

Susan went back inside and listened for the next two hours to stories of misuse, abuse, gambling debts, and in one instance theft. She could not believe her family would do this, especially when everyone in the Bowen family knew Great-Aunt Sarah's story. The hardship and sorrow over what she lost in the war was now tarnished with these indiscretions.

"It seems we are not going to have a lot of choice on the school then, are we?" Susan asked.

"I'm sorry, Susan, but no, we aren't," Ida answered.

"Well it could be worse. It could be a total stranger trying to rent the school," Susan told them.

"Susan, he seems very nice, and handsome, too," Angie said.

"He's an excellent doctor. It appears the politics of a larger hospital were not what he wanted and he was unable to accomplish what he intended with his practice. From our conversation today, Dr. Benjamin believes here he will be able to inform his patients, give options for treatment, and allow them to be involved in their care," Susan said.

"He has an open mind when it comes to our healing practices, Susan," Ida told her.

"Yes, and that was the biggest surprise of all when I went to work at the hospital in Savannah. He openly suggested natural healing in some cases. It almost cost him his job," Susan said.

"His car is nice, too," Angie said, and then smiled.

"Well, I like him, and he can stay with us so you two can talk. Susan, you were always the one who had the greatest interest in the school when no one else cared. You seem to have the touch your Aunt Sarah had, and that is something special," Ida said.

"I will see what he has to offer financially. If he will be good on his word about the school we might be able to work out an amicable deal," Susan responded.

"Who knows, you might work something else out, too," Aunt Ida said as she got up and headed for the kitchen.

"Aunt Ida! Our relationship is purely professional," Susan said before looking at Angie.

Ida turned and faced Susan. "I saw the way he looked at you, Susan Jane. You might be fooling yourself but his feelings aren't all professional. You be careful on how far you are willing to go with yours," Ida warned Susan.

Susan sat for a moment and looked at the bottom of her coffee cup. She had never thought of Dr. Benjamin in any other context.

"What do you think, Angie?" Susan asked.

"Does he dance?"

Bill finished packing his things at Mary Mayes', paid his bill, and headed back to the Bowen farm. He liked them—good people, honest folks—and it was nice to see Susan again. Bill smiled and thought about how he had a crush on her when she worked at the hospital. She saved his bacon more than once in Savannah. She had an uncanny knowledge of when something bad was about to happen. Susan's quick actions had saved lives and he would be forever thankful to her. He would make a decent offer for rent and hoped Susan would work for him. He couldn't pay much but was happy to have the help in a town where no one knew him yet. He wondered if Susan was still having nightmares. Bill turned on the radio and listened to "Indian Summer" by Tommy Dorsey. He then drove to a place he hoped to call home.

CHAPTER SIX

Tuesday, 1940
Honolulu, Hawaii
Christmas Eve

*L*arry sat on his balcony, in brown shorts and a tan Hawaiian shirt, with a glass of red wine. He enjoyed looking at the Christmas lights that had been hung on the palm trees and around balconies in his building. He looked over the article he had written on the London Blitz in September. He decided to take a harder line on Hitler and America's total blindness to what had been happening overseas. He had read stories about the murder of the mentally insane and the work camps, if that was what they truly were. If Great Britain could be attacked by Germany how long would it be before Hitler set his sights on America?

He closed his eyes as the breeze hit his face. It was just enough to make his time outside pleasant tonight. Larry had talked to his family earlier in the day with Christmas wishes and made sure his packages all arrived. His mother said she had sent papers that needed to be signed since the reading of the will. She was vague and didn't go into any detail when he questioned her.

He leaned back in his chair, listening to Christmas music sung by Dinah Shore and Frank Sinatra. He had settled into island life, loved his job, his boss was great, and he had been given freedom with his stories. Larry had been thinking frequently about his grandfather and the last day he saw him alive. He stood, went to his bedroom, and found the envelope in his top bureau drawer. Larry walked to the kitchen and poured another glass of wine before he returned to the balcony. He took the necklace and note outside. He needed to seal

the note or what was written on it could be lost or destroyed. There was something at the paper he could use to make sure that didn't happen. *I promise. Sarah.* Promise what? Why would anyone not finish explaining? Larry picked up the necklace and looked at the back. SJB, S for Sarah, B for Bowen, J could be for many names.

As Larry continued to look at the necklace the scent of lilacs surrounded him. Larry sniffed and looked around. There were no flowers inside and the only thing outside were palm trees. He stood and walked to the railing to make sure and found only plants, no flowers. He looked at the stone—pink, some type of quartz. He would see if he could find the significance of the stone. Larry sat back down and held the necklace in his hand. He tried to understand why these two items were so important to his grandfather but he would honor his last request and keep them safe and close. Who knew, there could be a story here.

CHAPTER SEVEN

Tuesday, December 31, 1940
New Office of Dr. William Benjamin

Susan, Angie, and Bill cleaned, painted, and went through old files. The women helped Bill move furniture and set up a waiting room and exam rooms. Bill had been good on his promise to Susan, and rooms had been set up at the back of the building so they could reopen the school. She helped her aunt and Angie bring all the herbs they had preserved in the root cellar back to the school. The open fireplaces had been replaced with gas heaters and they worked well today.

"Susan, did you hear Bill laughing at us?" Angie asked.

Susan looked in the mirror at the scarf around her head and the old work clothes that were her uncle's. "Guess he isn't up to date on the newest fashions," Susan answered.

"Girls, I am going up to the house to check on the folks. Susan, there is another letter at the house for you from your friend Judy," Ida told them.

"I'll pick it up later, Aunt Ida. I now owe her two letters," Susan said.

Susan watched Bill bring in box after box to his new office and begin to unpack. She thought about asking to help but remembered her aunt's warning and walked back to where Angie was working.

"Angie, do you think your dad would build us a new warming cupboard?" Susan asked.

"Probably, we need some new shelves, too," Angie answered.

"Susan, can you come in here for a few minutes?" Bill called out.

"What do you need?" Susan asked as she headed toward his voice.

Bill looked up and smiled as Susan entered his office. "I found this behind a loose board in the floor. I think this may have belonged to someone in your family." Bill handed Susan a weathered medical pouch. "It's covered in dust just like you. I think that may be blood on it, too."

Susan took the worn pouch but didn't open it. "Thanks, I will look at it later," she told him.

"If we keep working like this I will be able to stop making house calls and we can see patients shortly after the first of the year. That reminds me, I will be up to check on Ethan and Deanna before I go home. I am not happy with the coughs they both have and they aren't drinking enough fluids or eating properly," Bill's voice showed concern.

"I know; they are so stubborn. Angie, come and look at what Bill found," Susan called.

Angie walked into the room and looked at the pouch. "Has this been here all this time?"

"I guess," Susan told her.

"Hello, Bill, what's up? Did you know there is a dance tonight for New Year's? If you would like to go I would be happy to show you the Lindy, if you're game," Angie told him.

Bill began to laugh and smiled at Susan. "I think I might be free for an evening of celebration for a new year and a new life. Susan, you'll join us? Doctor's orders, no being alone on New Year's Eve. I will pick both of you up, say around eight," Bill said, not allowing either one to back out.

"That will be great. I love to dance!" Angie said in an excited voice.

Susan wasn't in the mood to go out but she would not disappoint her cousin. Bill was aware of the importance of this day and why she had nightmares. It was the same reason the big house remained closed.

They finished what they could and grabbed their jackets to head home. Bill had left earlier and drove up to check on Ethan and Deanna. They met him at the house.

"Susan, I will be back tomorrow to check on them. I have no problem with them wanting to use natural practices at this point in their lives. Tell Ida it will be fine. I am still concerned about them," Bill told her.

"Is there anything we can do to help right now?" Susan asked.

"No, sometimes their state of mind will be the final decision on whether they get well or not. Have you got a few minutes?" Bill asked Susan. He picked up their coats so they could go outside for a private conversation.

"Bill, I don't. . . . " Susan started.

"Susan, I know you don't want to go out tonight, nor do you want to talk about what causes your nightmares. There was nothing you could have done, and if you had been home you would be dead too. You need to talk to someone eventually about what you are feeling and face what happened to your family. Then maybe the nightmares will begin to fade away," Bill told her.

"Angie talks too much," Susan responded.

"No, she loves you and worries about you." He reached out and took her hand. "Susan, I am here if you want to talk. I care about you." Bill leaned in and kissed Susan on the side of her face.

Bill watched Susan's face turn a pleasant shade of red.

"Guess I better go get ready. We have a long night of dancing," she said.

usan turned and looked across to the big house that once belonged to her grandparents, James and Martha. Susan's parents built their home down the road from the big house. *Too many memories*, her father used to say. She had been out with friends at a New Year's Eve barn dance her last year of school. She returned to find her grandparents' barn on fire, the bodies of Uncle Leonard and Aunt Leona outside. As help began to come along with the sheriff, Susan found her father shot on the steps of the big house and her mother inside hurt, bleeding. Susan and the rest of the family did all they could to save her mother but in the end she died in Susan's arms. Susan's brother and two sisters were gone that night to stay with friends or they would all have been dead. James and Martha had been in the ground less than two years when this happened. The nightmares started a week later and had continued into her adult life. She knew Bill was right but Susan always blamed herself for the deaths. Her parents had offered to be chaperones but Susan talked them out of coming. If they had, they would still be here now. Those responsible were escaped prisoners who were caught and hung.

The Bowen family had had their share of misfortune and pain but always made it through. Susan was proud of what she had accomplished in her life but maybe the reason she traveled was to run away from what needed to be faced. She had not found the right person to share such pain and sorrow. Susan worried that person did not exist.

1940
John's Hangar
Leland, Mississippi
New Year's Eve

*D*ealer was about to win her fifth hand of the evening when she looked up at the clock and saw there were about twenty minutes before 1941. The heater in the hangar had kept the chill out and made the night more enjoyable. The barrel outside the hangar burned for those not interested in poker and more interested in drinking moonshine.

"Raise two bits," Lewis told her. "I think you're bluffin', girl. No one is that lucky."

"I'll see your two and raise two more," Dealer said, never blinking an eye.

"Call," Lewis answered. He turned over a full house. He laughed and reached for the pot.

Dealer smiled and showed a straight flush, royal flush. She took the pot.

Laughter broke out all around the table.

"Damn it, Butch! That is the fifth hand. How can she do that?" Lewis asked.

"Luck, brother, luck." Butch told him. He opened two beers and handed one to his daughter.

Dealer had been drinking since she was old enough to fly. Beer was her drink of choice. *Bud Chandler can keep his moonshine*, she thought. The radio was turned up and the countdown started. Dealer thought about the private charters she had suggested to her father. The conversion of the Waco for those charters had taken them out of the red and into the green with the bank.

Three, two, one . . . Happy New Year!

CHAPTER EIGHT

Friday, 1941
Waynesboro
Valentine's Day

Susan and Angie closed the School for Natural Healing for the night. Since Dr. Benjamin had opened his doors the extra money had helped them reopen the school. Many of their students had returned.

"Angie, I have to help Bill tomorrow morning for a while, and then make some community visits before I come home. Can you make the lesson plan for next week before you go to work at the hospital?" Susan asked.

"I can do that. I work the night shift,"Angie answered. "It's a good thing Mom made these aprons."

"I had forgotten about how bad some of these herbs stain," Susan told her.

"Are you going to stay and finish the charts for Bill tonight?"Angie asked.

"No, I'm heading home. I have to be here early, but I will walk with you until the road splits," Susan answered. "When did you say you work at the hospital?"

"I work this weekend," Angie told Susan.

"I work Tuesday and Wednesday at the hospital," Susan said. "Bill was thrilled about you being a nurse, too. It has made work at the office easier."

"Susan, you need to find more time for yourself. You do nothing but work. How about some fun? There is a dance next weekend and I know for a fact you are not scheduled to work. You can finish all your visits early. I will help get things ready for class this coming week. You haven't been out with me since New Year's. I saw you dancing with Bill. He likes you, you know?" Angie teased.

Susan didn't answer Angie and continued to put up herbs.

"I am coming over in Dad's truck to get you. I don't want any excuses. We're going. I will loan you a pair of my nylons if you go," Angie told her.

Susan thought about the offer of nylons for a minute. "Okay, I give in, we'll go out. I'll fix your hair for the nylons. Do you know who the band is?" Susan asked.

"I am not sure, sounds something like Miles' Band. It doesn't matter, we'll have fun," Angie told her.

"Angie, please tell me Eugene won't be there. I couldn't stand a night of him," Susan begged her.

"No, just Jerry. I promise, Susan."

"Good, I'm getting excited about going," Susan said.

"Jerry is such a good dancer," Angie responded.

"You have been seeing him for a while now. Any chance this is getting serious?" Susan asked.

"He works so hard and is determined to become a teacher. I don't think that I will get any marriage proposal until he can afford to take care of a wife," Angie answered.

"Good plan," Susan said and handed Angie her coat.

"What about you?" Angie asked.

Susan looked at Angie and shook her head. "There is nothing there, Angie. Bill is a wonderful doctor and we have had some good times out to dinner and dancing, but I am not ready to settle down. I want to travel again," Susan told her.

"You're not leaving, are you?" There was panic in Angie's voice.

"Not right now but I can't stay here forever. You and your mom can handle the school once things get back to where it is paying for itself. As long as Ethan and Deanna are alive I will stay," Susan said.

"They have been sick for so long this time, it doesn't seem either of them are getting better," Angie responded.

"I know. Bill went up there before class to check on both of them. I am surprised he isn't back yet," Susan said.

Susan shut the doors to the building but didn't lock them. The two walked arm in arm down the road to their homes, laughing until they saw Ida, Henry, and Bill walking toward them.

"No, please no," Angie said.

"Susan, Angie, I am so sorry. I did all I could do. They were both so frail," Bill told them.

"Girls, they went together, holding hands and peaceful," Henry said.

"Bill, thank you for being there," Susan said and held her cousin. "Angie, I'll stay, okay? I'll stay."

They all walked back to the house. Susan knew funeral plans had to be made. This would mean added time for her to remain in Waynesboro.

CHAPTER NINE

Sunday, April 13, 1941
Easter

*S*usan had just walked back to her house after Easter service in town followed by dinner with Angie and the family. She made excuses to leave so she could take a little time and walk around. She had always enjoyed walking the land, even as a child. Susan felt the need to check on James and Martha's house. It had taken some time for her to feel comfortable in her parents' home since she returned. She had put her own touch to the house—new curtains and furniture covers—which seemed to help. The land had changed over the years and the houses were closer, but still enough distance to give everyone room to roam, to breathe.

Susan changed into khaki pants, a yellow blouse, and tan sandals. She grabbed a light sweater and walked up to the big house and stood. She could not bring herself to walk up the steps. Aunt Ida checked here frequently and made sure that repairs were done. She and Uncle Henry had kept the house in good shape. The family hoped she would come back, live here, and raise a family.

"How about some company?" Bill asked.

Susan jumped at the sound of his voice.

"Susan, I am so sorry. I didn't mean to startle you," Bill reached out.

"Lost in thought and memory," Susan told him "Yes, please join me."

As they walked around the property Susan told Bill about the history of the land, the first house that was burned when Sherman's men came through Waynesboro. She went back as far as she could remember with the stories her parents and grandparents had told. She told him about the notes Martha made in the family Bible preserving the Bowen history.

"You and your family really do have quite the history here," Bill said.

"Yes, we do."

Susan looked at the sun and the clouds building. She took a deep breath and could smell the rain that would be coming soon. She turned and looked at Bill.

"I have a cherry pie at the house. How does that and coffee sound?" she asked.

"It sounds just fine to me," Bill told her. He took her hand and they walked back toward Susan's house. "I meant to ask you if you ever looked through the pouch. I am really interested to see if it belonged to your aunt."

Susan stopped. She hadn't thought about the pouch since December when she brought it home. "Oh God, I forgot all about it. The holidays, your office, the school, and then Ethan and Deanna's death . . . I never opened it," she told him.

"Well no time like the present, right? Let's go see what's in there. I'm certainly interested. What about you?" Bill asked.

Once they arrived at Susan's home she sent Bill to the kitchen to make coffee, and then went upstairs to get the pouch. When she returned to the kitchen she turned on the radio to Glenn Miller and his band was playing "In the Mood." There were two pieces of pie on plates on the table, and the smell of coffee still perking filled the room.

"I really like his music," Bill told her.

"Let's see what has been hidden from the world, shall we?" Susan told him.

They both sat down at the table. Susan tenderly opened the pouch and pulled out four books, a bell, and what looked like bandages made from old sheets. At that moment the kitchen filled with the scent of lilacs. They both looked at each other, not sure who should speak first.

"Do you smell that?" Susan asked.

"Yes," Bill answered, and then picked up one of the books and looked through it. "Susan, this is the *Botanic Family Physician* published in 1835. I have heard about this but have never seen one.

The coffee stopped perking. Bill stood, went to the stove, and brought the pot back to the table.

"Hot coffee for the lady," Bill said.

"Thanks," Susan replied.

Susan looked at the second book that was handwritten with drawings of flowers along with instructions on how to preserve and use them.

"Bill, look at this book. It was made by my great aunt and someone named Elise Bowen. Elise must have been her mother. My father had a sister named Amanda Elise. I need to look in Grandmother Martha's Bible," Susan told him.

Bill stood and walked to the back door and closed it. Dark clouds were gathering quickly and thunder could be heard increasing in intensity. He turned on the light. While Susan continued to look at the herb book put together by Sarah and Elise, Bill sat back down and picked up the last book and began to read. He stopped and looked at Susan.

"Susan, this is Sarah's journal. She started it the day she left Waynesboro with southern nurses to go help during the Civil War," Bill told her.

Susan was thrilled that she now had something that would bring her closer to the person she had tried to model herself after. The last book was, "The Women Who Travel in War," by Eric Samuel White, Jr., and Franklin Alfred Prichard. Susan quickly looked but didn't realize how important this book was to her and her family. She put the book back in the pouch and began to read to Bill the first few pages of Sarah's journal about a fight with Grandfather James and the need to leave and go heal. Sarah wrote about the women she left with, a little history about them and why they stopped at the farm.

Bill listened and looked at the sparkle in Susan's eyes with every word she read. "Does she say what the argument was about with your grandfather?" Bill inquired and looked up as the first bolt of lightning flashed across the sky.

"No, maybe she has written about it later in the journal. Bill, this is so wonderful. It looks like she has made notes about her feelings and the things that happened. I can't believe you found this. Thank you," Susan expressed her gratitude.

"Why are you thanking me?" Bill asked.

"Because if you hadn't come here and rented the school we never would have found all of this history," Susan said, and at that moment she leaned over and kissed him.

Bill looked at Susan, took her hands, and pulled her to him. The next bolt of lightning cut power and the lights went out. What started in the kitchen led to Susan's bedroom; clothes were left on the stairs, passionate kisses, and a night of holding bodies close in candlelight, exploration, endless pleasure, and release. A release Susan now knew was a reason to stop living in the past and hope for the future, a future without nightmares. As the power returned the radio downstairs played a slow song of which she could just hear the melody; it became their lullaby.

CHAPTER TEN

July 4, 1941
Honolulu, Hawaii

Larry finished his morning swim. Since Christmas he had become tanned and toned thanks to his favorite spot. He purchased his own surfboard and spent most of his off time improving his hang time. The redness in is hair had now turned blonde. Larry had a long list of beautiful women's names and phone numbers. Most were local but the beach brought tourists and more numbers. Once again he seemed to be at the right place at the right time. The military presence here was a story in itself. He made numerous friends on the base and had been promised information when it became available on upcoming military moves. Larry looked at the papers his mother had sent from New York on his kitchen table. His grandfather left him the controlling interest of the newspaper and placed him in charge of the trust that had been left for the Confederate nurse. Larry now felt the need to find the Bowen family and make sure the money would be used for the purpose it was meant. He never sent his inheritance paperwork back to his mother. He would give it to her when they came at Thanksgiving. He made arrangements to rent an apartment next door for his parents and Beatrice. It would be nice to see them, and plenty for them to see and do so he would not be expected to be their guide. The visit included a business trip for his father to the naval base, one he hoped to attend.

He had been invited to a party this evening at the home of Mr. Milton, owner of the newspaper. Dress would be casual, as always on the island. Larry had heard gossip at work that there were always movie stars at this party. He would love the opportunity to write about this gathering of names, but for once he would be part of the story. Larry would enjoy his anonymity and keep the spotlight away from his family and on those who made the news interesting.

Larry walked by his desk at his apartment and looked at the information sent to him about Great Britain and the United States placing embargos on Japan for petroleum and steel. Japan's war with China had been going on for a while; these embargos would not set well with Japan. A chill ran down his back.

He started toward the shower when he saw the items his grandfather had given him on the bureau. He stopped, picked up the necklace, and looked at the simplicity of the design. Larry knew he would have to take some time to do what his grandfather had asked. There must be relatives alive in that area of Georgia and people who would know who Sarah was and where the rest of the family lived. The next time he went home for a visit he would do some investigating, maybe go to Gettysburg and drive to Augusta. He would go after the first of the year.

CHAPTER ELEVEN

September 30, 1941
Leland, Mississippi

ealer returned to the Johns' hangar with two businessmen she had flown to Harrisburg. She tried not to listen to all the talk about America becoming involved in the war with Germany. Dealer stayed for a while and gave the needed maintenance to the Waco. She needed to check the other planes, too. Dealer had to get control of the dark feeling she had over all the talk of war.

"Dealer! I need to talk to you," Butch called.

Dealer stopped her work and went to the office.

"Dealer, girl, wipe the grease off your face," he laughed. "Thanks to you we have money in the bank and contracts for new acreage to dust."

Dealer took a rag out of her back pocket and instead of wiping off the grease she just added more to her forehead and chin. She closed the door to the office. "Paw, have you been listening to the radio lately? The men I brought back were talking about America becoming involved in the war in Germany," Dealer's voice quivered.

"Girl, you worry too much," Butch said. He walked over and tried to wipe some of the grease off his daughter's pretty face.

"Why shouldn't I worry? War would affect all of us," Dealer told him.

"Dealer, you're borrowing trouble; don't borrow trouble."

Dealer shook her head and walked out to refuel the Waco and prepare for tomorrow's flight. She couldn't shake the feeling she had about America going to war.

"Dealer, how long you gonna be here? Your maw is a fixin' dinner," Butch yelled at her.

"I can finish after dinner," Dealer answered.

"Your maw promised to make apple pie. I love apple pie," Butch said. He walked off whistling.

Dealer knew the conversation about war was over. She walked to the back of the truck and sat on the tailgate for the ride home.

CHAPTER TWELVE

November 12, 1941
Waynesboro,
Susan's Home

"Susan!"Angie called from the front door. "Are you home?"

"Come in, cousin. I just got home from the office," Susan told her. "Are you interested in a cup of tea? I have some leftover peach cobbler from dinner last night."

"That would be great," Angie said. "Where's Bill?"

Angie watched Susan put water on to boil for tea. Angie then walked into the living room and turned on the radio to Tommy Dorsey playing "All the Things You Are."

"He went to Augusta for a meeting. He should be back tonight. I just answered phone calls today, filed, and made a couple of poultices for Uncle Henry's back. Bill will be busy tomorrow," Susan answered. "He is seeing so many people here I have stopped working at the hospital to help out."

"I know that's the reason I am working tomorrow at the hospital, picking up your shift. You two have been seeing a lot of each other. What happened to 'our relationship is purely professional?'" Angie asked.

"I don't know if you can understand this, Angie, but it's something I needed. Maybe we both need it right now," Susan told her, and then looked at Angie as she put honey on the table.

"Well, you seem calmer and less tense. Can you sit down for a moment?"

Susan brought dishes to the table. "Angie, what's wrong? Are you okay?"

"I am fine. Where is the cobbler?"Angie avoided Susan's gaze.

"It's in the oven. Angie, are you going to tell me or just sit there and hope I'll guess?" Susan prodded.

The teapot whistled. Both women stood, Susan took the teapot and poured water into the cups. Angie found the cobbler in the oven, placed it on the table, took the spoon Susan handed her and dug into the cobbler.

"Susan, this is good," Angie kept her eyes low.

Susan sat down and reached over and took her cousin's hand. "Angie, tell me."

"You know I have been dating Jerry pretty steadily since you came home last year. We have talked about getting married even though he still wants to go to college," Angie looked at Susan.

"Well, have you set a date or is it still just talk?" Susan asked and smiled at Angie.

"I'm late," Angie told her.

Susan didn't speak for a moment. "How late?" she asked.

"Six weeks," Angie answered. She knew Susan was trying to understand how this happened. She was a nurse and should know how to prevent a pregnancy. Angie also knew that Susan would never judge her.

"Does Jerry know?" Susan asked.

"No, but I am going to tell him," Angie answered.

"When?"

"Tonight, we need to make some serious decisions very soon."

"You're not considering . . . " Susan stopped.

"No, of course not. But I would prefer to be married when this baby is born," Angie responded.

"Well it sounds like an early December wedding is in the works then. Congratulations," Susan told her.

"Thanks, I am a little scared but happy; so many feelings right now," Angie said. "Will you help us with the wedding? I know it will be fast but you are really good with those things."

Susan started laughing. "I'll be happy to do what I can, you know that."

"I would like to get married, if it's okay with you, at the big house," Angie said. "Do you think you can do that?"

Susan sat for a moment, drank her tea, and enjoyed day-old cobbler. "Angie, I think it's time for me to sweep the ghosts out of that house. I'll get Bill to help me."

"I know it's asking a lot but there were so many good times there for all of us," Angie said.

"It will be fine," Susan began. "It's a beautiful home and it needs to live."

"What are you going to do with the house, Susan?"Angie asked.

"I don't know. I thought about a boarding house of some kind or a home for children," Susan answered.

"Good ideas. I will help you with whatever you choose to do with it someday."

Susan stood up, took the calendar off the wall, and found a pencil.

"What are you looking at?" Angie asked.

"You know, if Jerry agrees we could have a Sunday afternoon wedding on December seventh after church services. That would give me plenty of time to get things arranged—the house opened, cleaned, and decorated," Susan told her.

"I'll let you know in the next few days," Angie said. "A Sunday afternoon sounds just fine with me."

*S*usan had looked over the notes she and Angie made about the wedding. There would be flowers, the pastor, food; things would be kept simple due to the shortage of time. She stood and grabbed her jacket and headed toward the big house. Susan walked up to James and Martha's house and began her speech to the ghosts.

"Tomorrow will be my day to start living and so will you once again; there will be happiness and joy in you, no more room for sorrow," she finished.

Susan smiled as she returned home, thinking about Angie being a mom. Susan suspected Angie was experiencing morning sickness and wanted to check the remedy book of Aunt Sarah's to see what she used so many years ago. She finished her letter to Judy, including the wedding for December seventh. Judy's last letter was filled with information of her new love and a possible marriage proposal. Susan thought about the journal, made some hot tea, went upstairs, and dressed for bed. She crawled into bed and opened the journal to where she had stopped reading to Bill.

February 28, 1863

The more days we spend together the more I understand these women. Each of us has a reason for being here—we hope we will make a difference, be strong, and not waiver when the battles begin. There was some trouble today when four union soldiers tried to take more from us than we were willing to give. I regret not bringing a weapon, but Ruby and Maud saved us. I may have to practice later.

SJB

P.S. I hope Mack is well. I miss that twig . . .

March 1863, Empty home south of Greenville, North Carolina

We have found a home to set up for the sick. Leona found a huge root cellar. She is an amazing young woman who I feel carries a heavy burden.

The sick and injured have found us. Such horror I have never seen ... it will take all our knowledge to help these people.

Prayers tonight for James, Mack, the family back home, and Ethan so far away from Georgia.

Susan was surprised about the reference to Ethan. She didn't know he left Georgia during the war, and who was Mack? Leona? Could this be Aunt Leona? She would ask Aunt Ida and Uncle Henry; this family history needed to be kept for generations to come. She was excited, but focusing had become more difficult so she put the journal in the nightstand. A few minutes later she was asleep, dreaming of family past, present, and now future.

*B*ill returned home late from his trip to Augusta. He drove by Susan's house and intended to stop but saw that the house was dark. The meeting had been intense, tiring, and long. He nearly missed picking up his package from the jeweler. He parked and gathered his suitcase and the special package he brought back. He had an early morning at the office and there were a couple of house calls that had to be made in the afternoon. He went to bed with the thought of his purchase in Augusta and his physical need at this moment for Susan. The next time Angie worked he would show her his Christmas gift for Susan. Bill would make Angie promise not to say anything or a special moment could be ruined for him and Susan.

CHAPTER THIRTEEN

8:30 a.m., Sunday, November 30, 1941
Honolulu, Hawaii

*L*arry had been awake for more than an hour waiting for his father to call. Even though he had agreed to join him for breakfast he dared not show up until he was summoned. The phone rang and Larry shook his head. A moment later he walked into the apartment he had rented for them and joined his father at the table.

"Lawrence, may I speak with you for a moment?" Jefferson asked his son.

"Go ahead," Larry responded. He was thankful his mother and sister left early to go to the beach. He had always hated these types of conversations with his father.

"I have been invited next Sunday to a breakfast at the naval base. Your mother has indicated that she abhors these kinds of things and wishes to stay here. Would you be interested in joining me?" Jefferson asked.

Larry was thrilled to get an opportunity to be part of what might be a story, but played it easy so his father would not be suspicious. "I would be honored, Father."

Jefferson looked up at his son. "It will be a suit and tie meeting. I assume you still own one, though I have not seen you properly dressed since we arrived," Jefferson said.

"Yes, Father, I still own a suit and tie. I have no intention of embarrassing you or your name," Larry answered.

"I would say it is our family name, but since you have chosen not to use it I do not feel the need to worry about how it reflects upon me except this time," Jefferson told him.

"Fine, Father, what time and where?" Larry had had enough. He didn't understand why all their conversations ended this way.

"Next Sunday, December seventh, we need to leave by 5:30 a.m. sharp," Jefferson said.

"I will be ready, suit and tie. Do you have a shirt color picked out for me, too?" Larry asked.

This ended the breakfast conversation between Father and Son.

CHAPTER FOURTEEN

4:00 p.m., December 6, 1941
James and Martha's House
March 1863

> We are getting prepared to leave and go to Chancellorsville. Our work here is done for now and the ladies at the healing house can take over for us. We must travel on. I am still worried about Emma and her baby. She is not eating and will not rest when I ask.
>
> I have written too many letters for the sons who have died here. The ones we healed have gone back to join their units. Many have left letters and photographs to be sent back to loved ones.
>
> My happiest moment was when Mack found us.
>
> My deepest hurt was the attack of the four renegades on Leona. I am to blame for not listening to the warning Mack gave me. God forgive me.
>
> We must now wait to see how she heals.
>
> I have read the papers that Mack brought, thinking they were military. To my surprise they are from a reporter talking about nurses. Stories the nation will read. Mack must take them back. They have to be returned so others will know what sacrifices have been made and why we, as women, have chosen to travel and heal.
>
> SJB

*M*ack must have been a soldier, maybe a spy for the South . . . and young too. There were so many questions and no answers to any of them. Susan finished her tea and decided it was time to get back to decorating and preparing for the wedding tomorrow. The whole family had worked hard, including Bill. The house was clean, linens changed, wood in the fireplaces, and ghosts swept out the front door. There had been a good feeling today, a new start. Angie had been there all morning, but Susan sent her away to make sure her suit still fit and was not too snug. Jerry was happy even though he would have to put school off another year. The Bowens had come together to get this wedding ready in record time. There would be the usual music, singing, dancing, food, cake, and drink. Susan was at peace with all things at this moment. She prayed it would last.

"Well you look comfortable," Bill teased her. "I think we still have a few things left here to do before we can relax."

"I have been reading Aunt Sarah's journal. It is so interesting to know she thought to write her feelings down. Bill, you have been wonderful to help with the wedding," Susan said.

She stood, walked over, and kissed him on the cheek. "The school is doing great and there are more calls every day asking for enroll-ment dates. Aunt Ida has had to come and help teach all the extra classes we have set up."

"Susan, it's nice to see you at peace and ease in this house. I never thought you would be able to come back here," Bill told her.

Susan smiled at him. "That makes two of us. Enough of me; we need to finish. Tomorrow is a big day for Angie and I want it to be wonderful," Susan said.

"Will I see you tonight?" Bill asked.

"No, tonight I need to stay with the bride and keep her sane," Susan answered.

They both laughed.

10:00 p.m.
Susan's house

*S*usan sat with Angie and laughed about all the things they did growing up together. Susan had brought Angie to her home at Aunt Ida's request. She had said that Angie was following her around like a lost pup and she couldn't get anything done.

"Susan, stop making me laugh. We need to get to bed. I made Jerry promise to sit in the back of the church and leave early so he doesn't see me," Angie told her.

"You don't believe that old tradition, do you?" Susan asked.

"Why tempt fate? We need all the luck we can get," Angie answered, and then laughed.

"I am happy for both of you," Susan had tears welling up. "I just wish Ethan and Deanna were here."

"Me, too, and you stop that; we don't need swollen eyes tomorrow."

Both women finished painting their nails, pinned, and wrapped their hair. Angie fell asleep first. Susan took Sarah's journal out and began to read one more entry before she went to bed.

As Susan began to read she realized Sarah had not dated these entries.

Mack left to take the papers back. I will always be worried about that twig.

Leona refused to stay at Healing House with Edith Blake. She is such a strong young woman. We head now to Chancellorsville and the next battle.

Emma does not feel well so we have made a bed in the back of the wagon for her. Down the road we have had to stop the wagon. Emma's water is broken. I check to see if the baby is moving. I cannot find any movement. We must stop soon for her sake.

Have found refuge with Pastor Allen and his wife Barbara in a place called Gaston.

Must make tea for Leona before bedtime. The twins and Leona will stay in barn under watch of Maud and Ruby.

In the early morning hours Emma delivers Ruth, born too soon, too small to live . . . War touches all of us.

Left Emma with Barbara Allen and her husband, I will keep her note to her beloved Leonard. No time to mourn for her loss. We move onto those who will need us.

Susan began to realize that Uncle Leonard and Aunt Leona weren't really family. They played a part in the Bowen history she was just now learning. She had so many questions but they would have to wait. Susan marked her place and fell asleep, thankful she belonged to a family so strong and one that cared for the pain and suffering of others.

Leland, Mississippi

ealer could not sleep this night. She drove to the hangar and hoped the things she loved would give some comfort. She sat in the office and listened to "The Shadow" on the radio. Dealer looked out the window into the dark and listened to a strange wind that blew. Something bad was coming; she felt it and knew there would be nothing she could do to stop it.

arry stood on his balcony and smoked a cigarette before going to bed. He looked at the gray suit, white shirt, and red tie he had laid out for the meeting in the morning. He walked inside and looked at the heart necklace on the bureau. Larry held it once more and looked at the initials on the back. He walked over and placed it in the inside pocket of his grey jacket just before he turned out the light and went to bed.

CHAPTER FIFTEEN

5:00 a.m., December 7, 1941

*L*arry adjusted his red necktie and made sure there would be no complaint or criticism by his father this morning. He picked up his jacket and slipped it over his tall frame. He reached to put his cigarettes in the same pocket as the necklace, and then changed his mind. He placed them in his shirt pocket instead. There was a knock on his door.

I knew it. Father is always early. "Just a moment, Father. I need to get my keys," Larry told him as he opened the door.

Jefferson looked at his son. "You made a good choice this morning, Lawrence. I would have chosen a darker necktie."

"This is the only necktie I brought with me," Larry answered.

Once downstairs, both men were ushered into a military car that waited for them. The drive to the base would be a short one. They were checked through the gate of the Ford Island Naval Air Station and continued to their intended destination.

Once they were inside the large military house it became apparent this was what Larry had expected—a private breakfast meeting. He knew his mother was all too familiar with these types of dealings. There were some contracts made in private before they were brought to the forefront of the government. Larry's father had what the military needed: steel; and there was a price to pay for those needs. He knew the only story here would be what had been served for breakfast. Any report of conversation could result in men dressed in dark suits visiting his boss. Breakfast began promptly at 0630 military time.

"Jefferson, how is Jean?" the general asked.

"She is well, thank you for asking. Jean and Beatrice had beach plans today or they would be here this morning," Jefferson told him.

"The weather report I received indicates a beautiful day for their excursion," the general responded.

This banter went on for about an hour. Larry needed a cigarette before he was subjected to more uninteresting conversation.

"Gentlemen, if you will, excuse me for a moment. I need to step outside," Larry told the men at the table.

Jefferson nodded his head. The other men acknowledged as Larry left the table.

Larry exited out the side doors. As he walked toward the water on another beautiful morning Larry longed to be surfing. He was thankful for the opportunity that had brought him to Hawaii. Larry looked at the ships on "Battleship Row" and could see the men of the USS Arizona beginning morning duties. It was 0755 when Larry struck a match to light his cigarette, but before he could get the fire to his smoke the first bomb exploded. The match burned down and blistered his finger before he realized what had just happened. The screams of men began; voices gave orders; sirens, gunfire, fire, and thick black smoke rose from the ships being attacked. Larry tried to take in the horror that appeared before him. The planes that attacked the ships had familiar markings, markings he knew well from reports and photos at the paper. Japan had attacked Pearl Harbor. He started to turn around when the next bomb struck too close and knocked him to his back; light turned to dark.

The black smoke rolled across the base like night. Larry opened his eyes and could not believe what was before him. His head lay in the lap of a beautiful woman. She looked down with the bluest eyes; hair the color of the sun, her dress blue checked with small pink flowers. He could see the dress was stained with blood, but the scent of lilacs engulfed them. She leaned down, kissed him tenderly, and then placed her hands on his face. Her voice was soothing but with such need when she whispered in his ear.

"Wait for me. Promise that you will wait for me."

Those were the last words he heard as she faded away along with his sight.

12:00 p.m.
Leland, Mississippi

    *D*ealer had received no comfort from her stay at the hangar during the night. She would apologize to her maw about missing church services later. She decided that the only place she would feel safe and work out these thoughts, these feelings, would be in the air. The freedom of flight was her refuge. She had finished the preflight check and crawled in the pilot's seat. The only noise now was the sound of the motor as she taxied the piper down the runway and headed for open sky.

    "I'm safe now."

1:00 p.m.
Waynesboro, Georgia

    "*S*usan! Hurry, we need to get to the big house. We only have an hour before the preacher and Jerry will be there!" Angie was almost screaming.

    "Angie, stop! I already have everything there. I took your clothes and mine up there before we went to church. We have plenty of time. There is enough family there, we'll only be in the way; it's all done. Nothing is going to go wrong today," Susan said and wrapped her arms around Angie.

    Susan let go of Angie and headed upstairs to gather her makeup. Angie walked to the back door and looked at the clouds building to the north. "I hope you're right, Susan."

Ford Island Naval Air Station, 9:00 a.m.

    "*L*awrence, Lawrence, wake up," Jefferson shook his son's shoulder.

    Jefferson's face and clothes were covered in black soot from the search for his son. He thought Lawrence had been killed when the attack first began. Jefferson called his son's name, searching desperately in the thick smoke from the burning ships. In the midst of the battle Jefferson was concerned he would not be able to find his son; panic had begun to set in when the scent of lilacs calmed him. It was at that moment he turned and found his son away from the water in a safe place. Jefferson obtained help and had his son moved inside where he sat thinking about all the stories Lawrence had written about a possible attack—stories no one seemed to be interested in reading, including him, and no one believed; now the skeptics had been proven wrong and what would be the cost in human lives? Jefferson thought about the war in Germany and wondered if Hitler would take this opportunity to declare war on the United States.

Jefferson was relieved when Lawrence began to speak.

"I promise . . . I promise," Larry repeated.

"Lawrence," Jefferson responded.

Larry opened his eyes to his father bending over him. He rose up on his elbows and looked around at the chaotic sight before him. He looked at his father's face and realized there was actual concern in it. Larry then sat up and checked his surroundings. He was back inside where breakfast had been served.

"Father, did you see her?" Larry asked.

"Who, Lawrence?"

"Did you see the woman who helped me?" Larry returned the question.

"Lawrence, you were alone when I found you. Are you hurt? I could not find any injuries," Jefferson asked. He was concerned with the talk of a woman who helped his son.

"No, I don't believe I am hurt, just knocked off my feet. Father, I have to get to a phone," Larry told him.

"The lines are all tied up or dead due to the attack. We cannot leave the base. I'm worried about your mother and Beatrice. It seems the attack is isolated to the base, but how can we know for sure?" Jefferson's voice quivered.

"Damn it to hell. I have to get an outside line. I need to get this story out so the nation knows what's going on here," Larry told him.

"Lawrence, we need to help out here. There are men seriously injured and not enough medical personnel available. That will be your story that no one else on the island will have when you are allowed back into town," Jefferson told his son.

Both men looked at the injured being brought inside.
"What can we do to help, Father?" Larry asked.

2:00 p.m.
Waynesboro, Georgia
The Big House

Susan stood in her navy suit and shoes, her hair pulled to one side with a simple clip. She wanted all eyes on Angie today. They were in the back bedroom where Angie finished last-minute concerns. Angie was beautiful in her tan suit with shoes to match. She had fussed with Susan about getting her seams straight and demanded Susan fix her hair in a chignon. *Pregnant brides can be so irritating at times,* Susan thought. Aunt Ida was dressed in her Sunday best as she walked over and placed a cream-colored net with matching bow in the back, over her daughter's face.

"Something old . . . Grammie Deanna's pearl necklace and earrings that Gramps Ethan gave her; something new . . . my suit; something borrowed . . . Susan's Bible; and something blue . . . my garter,"Angie said out loud to them.

"Here is the sixpence from your father for your shoe." Ida then looked at her daughter with loving eyes. "I love you."

"Mom . . . I," Angie stopped before the tears began to fall.

"I am going out to sit with everyone. It's time," Ida said, and opened the door. "Henry, I think we're ready."

Susan walked over to a special box, opened it, and then turned and handed a bouquet of white roses to Angie.

"Where did you get these?" Angie asked.

"Not me. Bill ordered them, his part of the wedding," Susan answered.

Susan held a smaller bouquet of red roses as they started out the door to a wedding march being played by family.

Henry, in the only suit he owned, took his daughter's arm. "Well, girl, let's get on with it, shall we?" he asked Angie.

Angie smiled and kissed her father on the cheek. "I'm ready," she said.

A few minutes later Angie and Jerry stood in front of Pastor Mims. As vows were exchanged Susan looked for Bill, who stood in the back. Susan had mixed feelings about him and their relationship. He was a good man, a good doctor, but she was not sure she loved him and worried about his feelings toward her. She should slow things down; it was time to start traveling again.

"May I have the ring, please?" Pastor Mims spoke to Susan.

"Oh, yes," Susan responded and handed him the ring.

Angie gave Susan her bouquet. Matching gold bands were placed on the third finger of left hands, with promises of love and fidelity. Pastor Mims smiled and began his final words after a short prayer for God's blessings on the couple.

"By the power invested in me by the state of Georgia and as your pastor, what God has joined together let no man put asunder," he said.

There were a number of Amen's from the crowd as Pastor Mims raised his hand over the couple.

"I now pronounce you husband and wife. Jerry, you may now kiss your bride," Pastor Mims finished.

A cheer erupted as Jerry kissed Angie, rather passionately.

They turned around to greet everyone when the front door of the house burst open and Dale Peak, a neighbor down the road, ran into the house.

"WE'RE AT WAR! THE JAPS ARE BOMBING PEARL HARBOR!"

1:00 p.m.
Leland, Mississippi

Dealer had been at peace for the last hour when she decided to go back. She made her usual bank and flew over the hangar. She saw numerous trucks, cars, and people who stood looking up.

"There she is; everyone get a towel and start waving," Butch told them.

Something is wrong . . . terribly wrong, Dealer thought. She brought the plane in as safely and quickly as possible, and then taxied to the hangar. When the propeller stopped she jumped out to see what all the excitement was about.

"Paw, what is everybody doing here?" Dealer asked. Jinny walked up and put her arms around her daughter. Dealer could see her mother and several other women had been crying. "Maw, what's wrong? Who's hurt?" Dealer asked.

"Deelyn, Pearl Harbor has been attacked by Japan. We're at war," Butch told his daughter.

"Maw, Uncle Sonny; where is he?" Dealer asked.

"He is on the USS Arizona," Jinny said and continued to cry.

Dealer held her mother. She watched as everyone headed back to the hangar. They all gathered around the radio that gave what news it had received from a place far from Leland, Mississippi.

10:00 p.m.
Big House
Waynesboro

*S*usan sat in front of the fireplace in the main room of the big house thinking about the day. Family and friends had gone to their homes to listen to the radio for more news on Pearl Harbor. Jerry and Angie left to take a very short honeymoon. It was hard to watch Angie cry on her wedding day because Jerry said he would be signing up as soon as they returned to join the fight. There would be a lot of the Bowens, Longs, and other men in the community who would sign up over the next few weeks to go and fight. War—our family had been involved in every war since 1863. She leaned back, took a quilt, covered up, and listened to Artie Shaw's "Dancing in the Dark."

*B*ill could see Susan through the screen door as he walked up the stairs to the big house. He had gone home to get the ring he had bought for Susan. He felt now would be the only chance he had to salvage a little happiness. He didn't think it would be long before he would be called back into the service of his country. He had never told Susan about his previous life in the military; it was another time, and one he didn't wish to relive. He took a deep breath, opened the screen door, and walked into the main room.

"Am I intruding?" Bill asked.

Susan didn't get up. "No, please sit," Susan told him, and opened the quilt so he could sit close to her.

Bill sat down and put his arm around Susan's shoulder. "Quite the day, wasn't it?"

"More than I think anyone here had planned," Susan answered as she laid her head on Bill's shoulder and pulled her feet up under the quilt. "Bill, I thought opening the house and sweeping out the ghosts would correct all my problems. I thought Angie and Jerry getting married here would be a fresh start, give me a reason to stay and do something good with the house."

"And what makes you think that you still can't make something good here?" Bill asked. He kissed Susan's forehead and reached for the ring in his pocket.

"I have made a decision to leave. After listening to the radio and hearing about the shortage of medical personnel, it's the right time to do this."

"No, Susan, please don't . . . " Bill began but was cut off by Susan.

"There will be difficult times ahead for our country. The military will need nurses who are willing to travel. As soon as Jerry and Angie return I intend to join the service," Susan said.

Bill took his hand out of his pocket. At that moment the music changed and Frank Sinatra began to sing "This Love of Mine."

What happiness might have been salvaged now remained in the bottom of his pocket.

❀

4:00 p.m.
Pearl Harbor

"*L*awrence, over here!" Jefferson called to his son.

Larry looked at the injured men lying everywhere. A doctor and nurse had found their way to the general's home. The house staff had been gathered and instructed to assist the medical personnel. They were told to find all the sheets, towels, table clothes; anything that could be used as a dressing. First aid kits, alcohol (medicinal and drinking), witch hazel, anything usable—even regular needles and thread were brought to the doctor and nurse. There was so much confusion and the injured continued to be brought here instead of the hospital. These men were covered in oil, gasoline, bullet wounds, arms and legs that had been blown off. The man at Larry's feet was burned beyond recognition.

"He's gone. Move on!" the doctor shouted at him.

"What? No, he was . . . " Larry started.

Larry felt the firm grip of the doctor pull him away. He turned back to see the nurse cover the man with a sheet.

"Only God can help him, but there are others who we can help. Now move!" the doctor shouted.

"Where is the rest of the medical help? Doctors, nurses, aides—why aren't they here to assist?" Larry asked.

"Young man, stop asking questions and start listening to me," the doctor said.

"This isn't happening; it just can't be happening. If I survive this day I swear on the bodies of these men that I will make America aware of what happened here. The need for nurses and doctors will be great to get through the days ahead."

"Lawrence, please help me over here, please," Jefferson begged.

Larry made his way over the injured and dying to his father. He knelt down and began to follow directions given by the doctor to help keep the man in front of them from bleeding to death.

❦

11:00 p.m.
Leland, Mississippi

ealer sat on the front porch and looked at the sky. She now knew the reason for her feelings these last few days. Dr. Ballard came by and gave Maw a shot of some kind that settled her nerves down. She had never seen her cry so much. Dealer was very glad tonight that her brothers weren't old enough to go to war. Uncle Lewis' boys were her age and older. They would be going into town tomorrow to sign up. Dealer knew her paw would wait for the shot to work on her maw before coming outside to talk. A moment later she heard him walk to the front door.

"Deelyn, what are you thinking about?" Butch asked as he sat down next to her and watched his daughter stare into the heavens.

"A lot of things, Paw. This war is going to affect everyone here in Leland. I'm worried about the business," Dealer said.

"Girl, we are going to be fine. I'm worried about your maw. Sonny is her only brother. The information coming over the radio is not good. The chance he survived is slim."

"Paw, tell me you won't have to go to war," Dealer said and laid her head on his arm.

"No, got a bad back. I tried to get into the service years ago. They wouldn't take me. I don't see them asking now," Butch said and smiled.

"Good, I don't think Maw would make it if you had to leave. She needs you here, Paw," Dealer told him.

Butch could see the tears in his daughter's eyes. He wrapped his big arm around his daughter's shoulders.

"I ain't going anywhere. I can do more here and help out where I am needed. There will be things to do here, extra work when the men leave. I'm going to need you, too," Butch said.

"I know, Paw, I know," Dealer said.

Dealer looked up at the stars again. There had to be something she could do. She could fly a plane; that had to count for something, didn't it?

CHAPTER SIXTEEN

1941, New Year's Eve
Honolulu

Larry finished his fifth article about the bombing of Pearl Harbor. This article dealt with the experience he and his entire family were involved with that day. He considered a special series on the medical staff that would travel overseas should he become a war correspondent. He hoped to be assigned with a medical unit to see firsthand how they reacted and cared for the wounded. The radio in his office was playing "Blue Orchids," by Glen Miller. Blue Orchids and blue eyes—her eyes, the woman who saved him. He was aware his father thought he imagined her but he knew that woman had been there, made him promise to wait for her. Could she have been Sarah? Were the stories true? Why did she appear to him? Questions he had no answers for at the present.

He looked around the office at all the reminders to "carry your gas mask" or be fined. How things had changed so fast. There were now rumors of rationing food and products. He regained his thought and looked at the next article about Germany declaring war against America, four days after Pearl Harbor. This now placed our country in two theaters of war. Larry was aware there would be many hardships and sacrifices on the people. Due to the shortage of medical personnel Larry asked nurses and doctors to heed the call of the military. These articles would run back-to-back in the paper. Larry took a cigarette out, lit it, and leaned back in his chair. He was thankful that his mother and Beatrice had been safe during the attack. His father was surprised when they found them assisting at a Red Cross center. He closed his eyes and the memory of the men he tried to help that day rushed back. If there had only been more nurses, more doctors, maybe so many would not have perished. He looked out the window and thought about his plans for a simple New Year's gathering to-night—no party, just family.

Lois Banner, Larry's secretary, finished the last of the day's work when her phone rang.

"Larry White's office. Right away, Mr. Milton," Lois replied. She opened the door to Larry's office.

"Larry, the boss needs you upstairs and he said right now. Good luck, my fingers are crossed," Lois told him.

Larry crushed his cigarette and headed out the door. He hoped this was the answer to his request for overseas duty to report. He found it funny that he worked so hard to get here to a cherry of a job—the parties, women, and a life most reporters would kill for—but after the attack he had changed, everything had changed. He needed to go and report what would happen to so many men and women far from their home. He intended for those here at home to not forget the cost that would be paid to keep their freedom safe.

Richard R. Milton stood and looked out his office window. He wondered how his beloved Honolulu would ever re-cover. The last few weeks had been trying on everyone at his office. Richard had relaxed the dress code for everyone since the attack. It had seemed to help with all that had happened. He was business; therefore, suit and tie remained standard. In his sixty years he never believed another country would attack America. Difficult decisions regarding the war and who should report it must be made. That deci-sion was his alone. The knock on the door and the man behind it was one of those decisions.

Larry stood outside the office door of Mr. Milton. He knew of a thousand reasons why he should be sent overseas. He hoped the man who controlled his future would listen.

"Come in, Larry," Milton said.

Larry entered and shook his boss's tanned hand. "How are you doing today, sir?" he asked.

"Fine, Larry, would you please sit down? Drink?" Richard asked.

"If you are having one, then yes," Larry answered.

As Richard stood to get them a drink Larry looked at his boss's full head of gray hair and the straightness of his six-foot posture. He knew this man played tennis on a regular basis. His steel blue eyes had seen much in his life, which now included the attack on his home.

Richard returned with a bottle of whiskey and two glasses. He looked at Larry. "I hate Scotch," he said, pouring them both a drink. "Larry, I have read your request to become attached to the military as a war correspondent. Your report from the naval base during the attack was impressive and well presented. The fact that your entire family became involved will hit home with our readers here and in the states. I have spent many nights since the seventh thinking about what I should do and who I should send into this war. It is obvious to me that you are that man. I did receive a letter from your father asking me not to send you," Richard said.

"Sir, I . . . " Larry began.

Richard raised his hand. "Larry, you should know by now that I am not inclined to be swayed by the words of others when it comes to my employees. This paper will miss you while you are gone but your job will be waiting when you return, and you will return. You will have three weeks to get your affairs in order. I will have your assignment and who you will report to by then," Richard told him.

He finished his drink, and then stood and walked over to Larry, who also stood.

"Good luck, son," Richard shook Larry's hand. "Be careful and keep safe."

"Thank you, sir. I will make you and the newspaper proud."

"You already have, Larry, you already have," Richard told him. "Now get out of my office and go take care of business. Don't forget your gas mask."

Larry left with a smile, excited about the experiences to come. Now the only problem he had was telling his family. He was angry his father tried to interfere but after what happened on the naval station he understood. Their conversations had been more civil with fewer arguments, and this had made him happy. He would wait to see what the mood of the family was tonight before he told them he was going to war, a family tradition that he would proudly continue.

8:00 p.m.
The Big House
Waynesboro

$\mathcal{S}$usan had finished setting the table and would light the candles just before dinner. She had prepared a nice meal and went into town earlier in the day for a bottle of wine. At the small breakfast table she sat and looked over the enlistment papers. She had filled them out and was ready to take them back to the Red Cross office in Waynesboro. Susan held off for a few weeks due to the holidays and the fact that Angie was not dealing well with Jerry leaving so soon. He and Eugene would be shipped out to San Diego in a few days. The last three weeks had been difficult for everyone in the Bowen and Long families. Bill had become distant after she told him she intended to join the military. Susan had some comfort knowing that he would be here to take care of the people in Waynesboro and watch over Angie until the baby came. Aunt Sarah's school would remain open as long as there were students. If it closed it would be because women were needed in the work force.

She gathered the papers and put them away; tonight it would be just the two of them. Susan looked at the clock; Bill would be there in ten minutes. She checked to make sure dinner was done, and then went upstairs to dress for dinner. She felt bad about the last time they were in this house together. She hoped they might be able to rationally discuss her decision to leave tonight at dinner. Susan brushed her hair to the side and put a small clip in it, adding the final touches to her makeup. The lavender-colored dress was form-fitting, low-cut. Finally, a light spray of perfume . . . lilacs.

$\mathcal{B}$ ill walked slowly to the big house. He had put the ring in his pocket and hoped Susan would listen to him. Maybe she would change her mind after he proposed. Bill started to knock on the door but Susan opened it first. She smiled at him.

"I hope you're hungry," Susan said.

Bill stopped and took in the full view of Susan. He wanted to hold, touch, and kiss her entire body at this very moment. He knew his physical reaction to the site of her would not wait until after dinner.

"Dinner will have to wait, at least for a while," Bill answered. He then led her upstairs and left all of the night's preparations suspended in time. Bill was surprised and pleased as Susan allowed him to slowly undress and make love to her.

Several hours later the sound of a distant chime made Bill look at the clock; it was after midnight. "Susan, what would you like to drink?"

"There's wine downstairs," Susan said, and threw a towel at him as he left.

Bill walked downstairs and found the bottle of wine and two glasses Susan had placed on the table. The radio upstairs was playing "You and I," by Glen Miller. Bill thought this song was appropriate at the moment and felt now would be the perfect opportunity to propose. He returned to the bedroom wearing the towel around his waist.

She smiled at him. "I don't think pink is your color."

"Oh, I don't know. I like pink," Bill said.

He sat down and poured two glasses of wine and handed one to her. The music changed to "Stardust," by Artie Shaw.

"Susan, you're so beautiful," he told her.

They touched glasses and drank. Susan blushed and turned away for a moment to adjust the volume of the radio. Bill reached in his jacket and placed the small black box under the pillow.

"I have always thought you were beautiful," Bill began. He sat his glass of wine on the floor. "I now know that what I felt for you then is the same feeling I have now. I fell in love with you the first time we met. I love you. I don't want you to go. Please stay and be my wife." He opened the black box.

S usan looked at the ring. She tried to control the anger building inside, not at him but at herself for letting their relationship come to this moment. Aunt Ida's warning rang in her head. She had not seen this coming and now Susan faced what she had known from the beginning. She did not, nor would she ever love him.

"Bill, I, I don't know what to say right now," Susan began. "I don't . . . "

"Susan, would you please think about this, give me a chance? I know we can make this work. I love you with my entire being. Please," Bill begged.

Susan sighed and looked at this man who said he loved her. "Give me a few days to think about this."

Bill leaned in and kissed her. "I love you."

Susan never answered. She closed the lid on the box. She hated herself for what had just happened. The last thing Susan remembered was Benny Goodman's "There'll Be Some Changes Made" as Bill wrapped his arms around her in a loving embrace for the last time.

CHAPTER SEVENTEEN

January 9, 1942
Augusta, Georgia

Susan drove to Augusta to meet Angie and Jerry in Uncle Henry's truck. Angie had asked her to come for support. Susan dreaded the drive back to Waynesboro with a pregnant new wife whose husband had been shipped off to war. Angie's hormones had gone haywire with the pregnancy. Her own brothers now ran away whenever she approached the house. Susan had been unable to find the herbs necessary to help with Angie's mood swings. She had bought ginger root for her nausea and chamomile tea to help keep Angie calm. The second reason for going to Augusta was to return the enlistment papers. Bill had too many friends at the Red Cross back home. The last thing she needed was for his phone to ring off the hook over her enlistment or word to get to her family before she had the opportunity to tell them. Susan knew after this week she would have to tell the family. Bill had been very patient over the proposal and her reluctance to give him an answer. She knew that was not going to last much longer. Susan found the address Angie gave her and was relieved to find a home, not a boarding house. There were so many men leaving tomorrow that all the rooms in town were filled. Susan saw Angie almost tear the door off its hinges as she drove up to the house. She knew Angie had probably been standing there for the last half hour, waiting.

"Susan, I am so glad to see you." She began to cry.

Susan wrapped her arms around her cousin. "Angie, it will be okay. We are all going to get through this together."

Angie was now about thirteen weeks pregnant. She still fit into regular clothes with the exception of a slightly larger top and an ever-growing temper at times.

"Are you sure about that, Susan?" Angie asked her. "Where is Bill? I thought he was coming with you."

"I didn't tell him I was coming. I want to do some shopping before we are forced to use ration stamps. I didn't want to drag him around," Susan made her excuses and hoped Angie would believe them.

Susan met the lady who would rent her a room for the night. Angie looked tired and Susan was happy when she said she needed a nap. Susan waited about thirty minutes and then left for the Red Cross. The line was not long and she was quickly called to a desk. The woman looked over Susan's papers. She had asked to be a task nurse. Task nurses would be sent overseas.

"You are exactly the type of nurse we need. I wish you had been here a week ago. We are sending a group out tomorrow. We have another group leaving in two weeks. Can you be here?" the recruiter asked.

Without hesitation, Susan answered, "Yes."

Susan shopped for the rest of the afternoon. She bought a gift for the baby even though she knew it was early. She went to see *Tales of Manhattan* with Henry Ford, and then stopped at the local diner for a cup of coffee. She sat at the counter thinking about what she had just done. There was an excitement she could not still inside. She must now tell Bill she could not marry him. Susan would tell her family she was leaving to go heal, like Aunt Sarah.

Susan had agreed to go to dinner with Angie, Jerry, and Eugene that night. She had finished dressing when Angie knocked on her door. She was beautiful. Pregnant women had such a glow that surrounded them. Angie had a smile, though Susan could tell she had been crying.

"Susan, are you ready?" Angie asked.

"I guess. I cannot believe I am spending the evening sitting across the table from Eugene," Susan replied.

"You are bad and going to hell. I am going to tell Mom on you," Angie said.

"Go ahead. What can she do? Lock me in the house?" Susan answered then laughed.

The four walked to a small restaurant in town. Susan listened to Jerry and Eugene talk about going to San Diego. Susan ordered a drink as soon as they sat down. *Liquor has to make the evening more tolerable,* she thought.

"I don't think we will be in the same unit after what happened at Pearl Harbor. There were entire family lines destroyed so I am sure we will not be together except through training," Jerry told them.

"Susan, what are you going to do to help the war effort? Bake cookies, collect cans, turn in your girdle?" Eugene said, and then laughed.

Susan had enough of Eugene; before she could stop she turned in the chair and looked him in the eye.

"You are such a jackass, Eugene. I would kick your balls off and hang them over a lamppost but I love Jerry and Angie too much to go to jail right now. You can kiss my ass," Susan told him in a loud voice.

The entire table became quiet and the people at the table next to them broke out in laughter. The soldier at the table turned around and looked at Susan.

"You tell him, sister. We could use a few like you in the army," he said.

"Well, I guess she told you, Eugene," Jerry told him and burst into laughter.

We all started laughing. That was the last time Eugene said anything ugly or out of place to Susan.

8:00 a.m., *January 10, 1942*
Train Station, Augusta

Susan stood back and watched Angie hold onto Jerry until the last minute. She held up well but Susan knew the ride home would be tearful. The whistle blew and the conductor called for all to get on board.

Jerry hugged and kissed Angie once more, and then ran off to where Eugene waved for him to come. Angie ran with the train so she could see him a few moments longer.

"I love you, baby. I will write, I promise. I love you. Take care of our baby," Jerry screamed to her.

"We love you, too . . . " Angie said as the train pulled out of the station.

Susan walked up next to Angie. "Are you going to be all right?"

"After the dinner conversation we had last night, I think so," Angie said. "Susan, if it hadn't been for you I think both of us would not have been able to do this today. Thanks. That was great."

"Let's go home," Susan said, and put a supporting arm around her.

They went back to the house and packed for home. Susan paid the lady for the use of the room. As Angie got into the truck Susan looked at the soda pop bottles filled with water.

"Angie, if you drink all that water, as you should, I will have to find a big tree down the road. There aren't that many gas stations or diners along the way home, you know that?" Susan told her.

"I know, and a big tree or small clump of bushes will do me fine," Angie brightly answered, waving a handful of tissues.

They both laughed; the tearful trip home was now filled with lighter conversation and talk of the baby.

"Susan, would you mind staying in the big house with me tonight? I don't want to spend this first night alone or at home," Angie asked. "We can build a fire and sleep in the main room like we used to do when we were kids. If you pull a mattress in there we can listen to the radio and stay up all night."

Susan knew well that Angie would be asleep long before midnight. "I have a few things I want to talk about, too."

"It wouldn't have anything to do with an emerald-cut engagement ring, would it?" Angie looked at Susan.

Susan almost wrecked the truck. She pulled off the road to finish this conversation. "Are you telling me you knew about the ring? And if so, why didn't you say something to me?" Susan asked.

"Because, Susan, Bill loves you, and he asked me not to tell you. I promised and I kept that promise," Angie said. "Did you say yes? He wants to marry you on Valentine's Day . . . oops! That is something I didn't promise to keep to myself."

"I don't want to do this here but we have to talk tonight," Susan said as she pulled back onto the road and headed for home.

"He wants to have four children, you know," Angie added.

Susan beat her head on the stirring wheel. She wished Uncle Henry's truck had a radio. "I will talk to you later about this."

"Okay by me," Angie answered. She then began to sing, "You are my Sunshine . . . "

Honolulu

*L*arry bought a package of cigarettes while his family picked up their tickets for home at the counter. His family had been very supportive of his decision. Mother and Beatrice were in the process of planning war efforts once they returned to New York. Larry and his father had become friends and closer since their ordeal at Pearl. Larry was sad that it took the death of so many men to make both of them realize what family meant and how silly their feud had been over the past years.

"Larry, I think we are just about ready to leave," Jefferson told him.

Larry looked at his father, who wore a baby-blue Hawaiian shirt and tan slacks. He smiled thinking about what his father's friends would say if they could see him at this very moment. Larry walked to the door where he could see the presence of the military close to the plane.

"Son, I'm not happy about your choice, but it's in your blood. Promise you will write or send word so I'll not worry so much," Jean asked him.

"Mother, I will send word when I can. I promise," Larry answered.

Jean kissed and hugged her son tightly.

Beatrice had tears falling. "You better not get yourself killed, you hear me?" She then hugged and kissed her brother.

"I will surely try not to get killed sis."

Beatrice and Jean walked away, leaving Jefferson alone with his son.

"I am very proud of you. Be safe and come home," Jefferson said. Then he did something he hadn't since Larry was a small boy; Jefferson hugged his son. "I will call when we get home."

"I'll be waiting," Larry said.

Larry stood and watched until the plane was out of sight. He then headed out of the airport and home to make arrangements for his apartment, car, and personal items until he returned from the war. Larry received a package with a list of items he would be able to take with him. He did not tell his family but he would be going overseas, as everyone else in his position, destination unknown.

Midnight
The Big House
May 1863, Wilderness Tavern

> *We have just arrived in Chancellorsville; we are late. There are so many men here injured. Ruby Belle has met an old friend, Mollie, who has given us instructions on checking the battlefields at night. We carry bells to let the enemy know nurses are on the field.*

That's what that bell was for, Susan thought, *safety.* She looked over at Angie and listened to the even breathing of her cousin asleep next to her on the mattress in the main room. The conversation over the engagement ring had stalled for the moment. Angie wanted Susan to marry Bill but she had to leave. She had told Angie a year ago she would not be able to stay forever. Angie was fond of Bill and had become protective of him. Susan felt if Angie had not become pregnant with Jerry's child she and Bill might have become a couple. Susan had put herself in the way of something that would have been a good match. She shook her head and went back to the journal.

> *All of us are holding up well. I miss not being able to clean myself on a daily basis, but we are all the same here. The weather is allowing us to find fresh flowers and roots to make teas.*
> *Leona is having her monthly cycles, which I am forever grateful for.*
> *I have walked to the main house where the surgeries take place. Dreadful, legs and arms are hacked off without the thought or care of what they are doing.*
> *We have met a doctor from Greenville—Dr. Theodore Bell; he is our friend and protector.*

Susan knew her aunt would have worried about a pregnancy from the attack on the young girl, Leona. She stopped reading and went to the kitchen for a cup of tea. There was the lightest scent of lilac in the kitchen. A chill ran across Susan's arms. This was the second time this had happened when the journal had been read. She returned and looked around the main room. Susan felt silly thinking the ghost of her dead aunt would appear. She sat down and continued to read.

A great general has been injured: "Stonewall Jackson," but we are not allowed to help.

Susan stopped and could not believe what she had just read. *Stonewall Jackson; it was not possible, was it?* she thought.

A man with an injured soldier arrived later, begging for help; he was turned away at the main building. I tried to get his attention but he did not hear me. Ruby Belle's voice carried farther than mine. We took the soldier to care for him. To our surprise, this wounded soldier was a woman.

Susan stopped reading, unable to believe what was written on this page. There was no information about women being on the battlefield other than nurses, wives, and in some instances prostitutes.

This man is a reporter from New York. He is Samuel White, my childhood friend; we had never met until this moment.

We talked for a moment; he is the man writing about nurses. I am forever thankful to Mack for returning his papers.

Susan marked her place and closed the journal. There was so much Susan did not know about her own family history, but hoped this journal would fill in the blanks. How was it possible her aunt and this man knew each other? She now had a name—White. The same name on the other book, the one about nurses who traveled and healed during the Civil War. Maybe she could make some inquires before she was shipped out. Surely this man had relatives still in New York.

CHAPTER EIGHTEEN

Monday, January 26, 1942
Leland, Mississippi

Dealer had been working on the planes at the hangar since dawn. Uncle Lewis had taken his sons to the bus station to see them off. He would not be the only father there sending sons off to war today. The ladder she was standing on moved, the wrench slipped, and she pinched her finger.

"Damn it, shit, hell!" she shouted and threw the wrench on the ground.

"Deelyn, watch your language," Butch told her.

"Sorry, Paw, I thought I was the only one here."

"Well you ain't, and a lady doesn't talk like that. How are you ever gonna find a husband talking like a sailor?" he scolded.

"I ain't looking for a husband and I wish I was a sailor," she said.

"Deelyn, I know what you're thinking, and your maw couldn't handle that right now. You need to think about her. We got the official letter today from the navy. Your uncle was one of the many men who were killed on the USS Arizona." Butch took a rag out of his back pocket and blew his nose. "Your maw needs you, girl, and don't forget that. I need you, too."

Dealer got off the ladder and walked over and hugged her paw. "I know but I feel so useless here. There has to be something I can do to help; there has to be, Paw."

"Well, unless the military decides to let women fly I guess you will have to just stay here," Butch said.

"You would let me go and fly planes?" Dealer asked.

"Well, if the military ever does that, pigs will fly, too. But yes, I would let you go," Butch told her.

"Paw, I will hold you to that promise," she told him.
Dealer now had hope, and that made her heart feel good.

Honolulu, Hawaii

$\mathscr{L}$ arry finished packing the duffle bag sent to him by the military. The list had limited him to what he would be able to take. The military would give him clothes; any civilian clothing would be sent home. He had said his goodbyes to everyone at the office. His car had been sold, a hold placed on his apartment, furniture and other personal items placed in storage. He had signed all the papers from Grandfather's will and gave them to his mother before she left. He made a will and gave it to his boss to keep. He told Mr. Milton it was his important papers, etc. Larry walked into his bedroom and picked up the necklace and note that he sealed at the paper to save the writing.

"Good luck charm? I guess I'll find out," Larry said out loud.

At that moment the entire apartment filled with the scent of lilacs. Larry smiled and placed the items in his pocket next to his heart.

Waynesboro, Georgia

$\mathscr{S}$ usan returned to her home from the big house after closing it. She had cleaned and covered furniture for days. Angie and Aunt Ida were too busy with the school and the office to take any notice of what she had been doing this week. Susan received a telegram a week ago advising her the date to report to Augusta had been changed to February second. She would report and take her oath before boarding the train, and then receive her unit assignment. Bill was pushing her now for an answer, and Friday she would give him one. Susan made tea and read the letters from her sisters about their husbands who had joined the navy. Susan's brother had not sent any word but she knew his sense of pride. He would join and fight. She would send letters to everyone, including her friend Judy, once she was assigned to a unit. They would understand her wandering gypsy spirit.

Angie received one letter from Jerry. He was tired, sore, and missed her. Angie still had morning sickness and probably would for a while longer, but the ginger root tea had helped. Tonight at dinner Susan would tell the family about her enlistment. She had to put her affairs in order this week, and that included Bill.

Dr. Benjamin's Office

*B*ill sat at his desk and stared at the telegram he just received. He was surprised the military found him so quickly. He must report to Augusta tomorrow for orders and instructions. This telegram had upset all of Bill's plans. He and Susan were to have dinner this Friday. She had promised to give him an answer. This telegram was not something he wanted to add to their conversation and wedding plans for Valentine's Day. Bill could hear Angie and Ida in the school. He stood and walked to the door.

"Angie, can you come in here for a moment and bring the schedule book?" Bill called out.

Angie walked into his office. "What can I do for you, boss?" she asked.

"Angie, I must leave tonight for an unexpected meeting in Augusta. This is something that I cannot refuse to do—business and medical issues of importance. I need you to reschedule all my appointments to Friday. If someone needs to be seen I would appreciate you or Susan seeing him or her. If it is serious send them to the hospital," Bill continued his instructions.

Angie looked in the schedule book. "Bill, there are only a couple of appointments tomorrow," she said.

Bill was glad to know that when he returned Friday it would be a light day. "Well, that helps me out. How are you feeling?" Bill asked.

"The morning sickness is better. Susan gave me some ginger root to make tea and it has really helped."

"Any word from Jerry?" Bill continued.

"Yes, I received another letter this morning but haven't had a chance to read it yet. Has Susan given you an answer?" Angie asked.

"She promised to give me an answer Friday," he said.

Angie smiled and walked off.

Bill would go to Augusta and see how much time he had before his life was no longer his. He walked out into the waiting room and looked around the office. He had accomplished so much in such a short time. He loved the people here and their way of life. His hope for a real home, wife, and children seemed to be slipping away. It now seemed there was nothing he could do to stop it with the arrival of this telegram. His marriage to Susan would be his anchor.

5:00 p.m.
Susan's Home

𝒮usan was upstairs going over the list of things she could bring with her. She would take only one dress with her, as she knew it would have to be sent back home. She had a recipe for soap she tucked in Aunt Sarah's journal, monthly cycle products, and a small book on herbs. She heard the front door open.

"Susan, Susan, where are you?" Bill called.

Susan hurried downstairs, not wanting Bill to see her packing. "I'm here. What's going on? Is there a problem at the office? Is Angie okay?" Susan fired questions at him.

"Whoa, slow down there. Nothing is wrong. I just wanted to come by and tell you I have been called to an emergency meeting in Augusta. I will be back in time for our dinner on Friday."

Susan saw Bill look at her left hand to see if she had put on the ring . . . she hadn't.

"We have a lot to talk about you know," he smiled.

"Bill, I . . . I want to talk about your plans, too," she told him.

"Good," Bill said and kissed her. "I'll see you Friday."

Susan walked out the door with him and watched as he drove away. She should've told him. *Why couldn't she just tell him?* "Damn it, damn it, damn it!" she shouted.

"Susan Jane, what did I tell you about cursing?" Ida said sternly. "Dinner's ready."

"I'm sorry, Aunt Ida," Susan said closing her eyes.

"You aren't going to marry him, are you, girl?"

Susan opened her eyes and looked at her aunt. "No, I'm not. And that's the problem."

"Susan Jane, I tried to warn you," Ida reminded her. "Come on; we can discuss all this over dinner. There is nothing ever decided on an empty stomach."

Susan wrapped her arm around her aunt and they turned and started walking.

"I made chicken fried steak," Ida said.

"Mashed potatoes and gravy, too?" Susan was excited.

"Of course, girl, and cherry pie."

"My favorite meal. I won't be able to walk home after this," Susan said.

"Well, there is always an empty bed you can sleep in girl."

When they entered the house Susan could see that Angie had already set the table.

"Did you see Bill before he left?" Angie asked.

"Yes, do you know why he had to go tonight?" Susan returned the question.

"No, he said it was some type of emergency meeting and he had to leave. I rescheduled the appointments with those who have telephones. We will just have to be at the office to catch the others," Angie informed her.

Uncle Henry, Josh, and Jacob came in, food was placed on the table, and all joined hands for the evening prayer. Comfort food was the best remedy for any problem. Susan hoped the cherry pie and coffee would ease her unexpected announcement to her family. After dinner the plates were cleared and pie brought to the table.

"Susan, I saw you up at the big house yesterday. What were you doing?" Henry asked.

"Closing the house, Uncle," Susan answered.

Ida looked at Henry and then her sons. "Boys, you two go out and check the cows. Don't come back till I tell you."

"Yes, ma'am," both said, got up, and left quickly.

Susan waited until the boys were gone and looked at her family and into Angie's face.

"I have joined the army. I will be shipped out to a base for training February second from Augusta," Susan announced.

"No!" Angie screamed.

Ida lowered her head.

Uncle Henry stood up. "Lord God Almighty, Susan Jane, what the hell are you thinking? Ain't this family suffered enough in the wars?" His voice was loud and filled with anger.

"Henry, stop yelling," Ida said, and wiped the tears from her face with the edge of her apron.

"Please, all of you stop and listen for just a minute to me," Susan begged.

Henry finally sat back down at the table. Ida got up and brought tissues to the table for her and Angie.

"Go ahead, Susan Jane, I want to hear what you have to say about all this," Henry told her.

"When I came back home I told all of you it would not be permanent. I have traveled to work before the war started. I have a wandering spirit. The army will be the opportunity I need to see the world and do my job as a nurse. The nursing shortage in the military is critical. Angie can help Bill at the office, and Aunt Ida, you can assist with the school as long as there are students. I will come back when the war is over, but I am going," Susan told them honestly.

Susan watched as her family tried to understand and make sense of her reasons to leave.

"Susan Jane, this is war. You are going to be in danger, possibly injured or killed," Henry said.

"I understand that and it is my decision to still go. I can help save lives. Please, all of you try to understand I have to do this," Susan continued.

"Susan Jane, I believe you are a lot like your Aunt Sarah. If you have to go then you have to go. I don't want you to but I will try to understand," Ida told her.

"What about Bill, Susan? What are you going to tell him? How can you hurt him like this?" Angie asked as tears ran down her face.

"I am going to tell him the truth, Angie. I can't marry him."

"But why can't you marry him, Susan?" Angie asked, her voice harsh.

"Because I don't love him."

*S*usan walked back to her house alone and upset at Angie. She had no right to be mad over her personal issues. What had happened between Bill and her was just that, between them. She never promised Bill her love or her life.

Susan needed a drink. She walked into the kitchen and found a bottle of whiskey. She took a small glass and poured a drink. She grabbed the bottle, walked upstairs, undressed, and got into bed. It had been a while since she drank liquor but now was the time. Susan reached over and picked up the journal and began to read.

May–June 1863

Samuel has spent several weeks with us. He is pushing me to tell him about Mack. I will make a story up that sounds good and believable.

This man is so handsome, tall, brown hair, and haunting green eyes, but he has a gentle side and has been a great help to us at times.

We are getting ready to leave to head to Middleburg for the next fight.

A colleague of Samuel's has come to our camp, but he was injured helping Maud. Samuel must now travel back to New York.

The morning he had to leave was very difficult for me. Should I tell this man I love him? Should I go with him? How can I let him leave . . . ?

He kissed me . . . then said for me to look for him, that he would return.

As I watched him leave, my heart became heavy . . . I do not have a good feeling.

Mack has come for another visit. I am so happy to see the Night Walker.

I knew it! Mack was a spy for the South and Aunt Sarah knew him. Susan finished her whiskey and turned out the lights. There had been no nightmares since she and Bill made love the first time, but tonight they returned, a warning of all the death to come.

CHAPTER NINETEEN

0700, Tuesday, January 27
Augusta, Georgia
Army Recruiter

*B*ill arrived at the designated time that had been posted on his telegram.

"Captain Benjamin, thank you for coming so quickly," the officer told him.

"I don't believe this telegram gave me much option, did it?" Bill answered the young officer.

"We are calling all reserves back, sir. You have a week to get your affairs in order and report back here for assignment. The next few days here you will be filling out papers. You . . . " the officer began.

"I thought I would only be here overnight," Bill's voice increased.

"No, sir, you will be here until Friday; maybe longer," he responded.

Bill finished what was expected, and then left the office angry and upset at this turn of events. He walked heavily to the corner coffee shop. Bill sat at the counter drinking a fresh brewed cup. He knew what his duty and responsibility were to his country. Bill worried whether Susan would marry him before he had to leave Waynesboro. He found a phone booth inside the shop and made a call to his office.

"Susan?" Bill asked.

"No, this is Ida Bowen," she replied.

"Ida, it's Bill. Where are Angie and Susan?"

"They are at the house. Angie isn't feeling well today and I offered to come check the office. I have a class in an hour to teach," Ida told him.

"I am going to be caught in Augusta until Friday late. Please have Angie and Susan reschedule all my appointments to Monday. I'll need to talk with the three of you when I get back," Bill told her.

We'll take care of things here. You take care of yourself and we'll see you when you return," Ida said.

Now what? Ida thought. She didn't feel it was her place to give him bad news. She walked into the classroom where Angie and Susan stood.

"Girls, Bill just called and said he is stuck over in Augusta and will not return until Friday late," Ida told them, looking at Susan.

Angie looked at Susan. "What are you going to do?"

"What can I do?" Susan responded.

"Susan Jane, he deserves to hear it from you. If he doesn't get back in time you will have to make a decision," Ida told her.

"I know, but what can I do? I need to leave Saturday morning. This is not working out as I had hoped. He said he would be back in the morning; what the hell is going on that he can't come home?"

"Susan, this is so unfair to both of you. Why can't you be normal like everyone else?" Angie asked.

Susan looked at her cousin. "Angie, I don't need this now, but if it will make you feel better I am not normal. Are you satisfied?" Susan's voice was short.

"Enough, both of you. I will not have this bickering. What's done is done; we cannot change it," Ida told both of them. "Susan Jane, you make up your mind about what you are going to do about Bill and we will abide. If you want me to tell him I will, or you can write a letter, but you will not leave this land until I know what you are going to do. You need to do the right thing, you understand?"

"I will, I promise, Aunt Ida. I'm sorry, Angie. Please understand I have to love the person I want to spend my life with, and Bill is not that man," Susan answered.

"I'm sorry, too, for the both of you."

CHAPTER TWENTY

Saturday, January 31, 1942

*S*usan placed her things in the truck while Uncle Henry waited. She had said her goodbyes to the boys before they left for the fields and morning chores.

"Just a minute, I need to do something," Susan told him.

Susan walked up to Ida and Angie. She gave the small black box and letter for Bill to Aunt Ida.

"I don't understand where he is, Aunt Ida. I waited up late for him. I have to leave," she told her.

Susan handed Aunt Sarah's pouch to Angie. "Keep this for me until I get back. I'm taking the journal with me."

"Susan Jane, it's fine. Whatever is keeping him away must be important," Ida said.

"I rescheduled all the appointments for Monday, nothing serious at the moment," Angie told her.

Susan held tightly to her aunt and cousin.

"You write to me, Susan. I can't take this with you and Jerry both gone," Angie's voice trembled.

"I will when I can, I promise all of you. Take care of Aunt Sarah's school and do whatever you feel is necessary, even if it means closing it again. I will understand," Susan told them.

Ida hugged and kissed Susan. "God bless and keep you until you return home. Say your prayers at night, girl."

Susan crawled into the truck. "Uncle Henry, would you take me to the family plot before we leave? I need to see them one more time," Susan asked quietly.

Henry started the truck and drove Susan to the family cemetery on Bowen land to say her goodbyes.

Susan walked where weeds had grown; the gate needed to be painted and the small stone markers of family laid to rest needed to be straightened. Susan would remind Uncle Henry to have the boys come and take better care of the family.

She stood, head bowed in reverence, for a moment. "I promise to make all of you proud. I will care for the sick, injured, and give comfort where possible."

The response from the dead was not heard in words, but with a slight breeze that reminded Susan of her mother's healing kiss.

*B*ill had hoped his recall to service would be streamlined and the mountains of paperwork completed by now so that he could return home to his patients and Susan. It soon became obvious nothing had changed in the military. Another phone call was necessary along with Ida's reassurance that everything in Waynesboro would be taken care of until his return. Bill was concerned that Susan had not been available for any of his calls but he would stop at her house when he returned. He now had a couple of hours until the next round of paperwork would be needed. Bill would take those hours and make good use of them. His first priority was to meet with an attorney and complete a will, then meet Dr. Small. Dr. Small had been suggested by the army doctor who had given him his physical. He told Bill that Dr. Small was old-school and believed in using nature to heal. When Bill called him he said he would be happy to see his patients while he was gone. Bill felt fortunate to have found a man who accepted natural healing along with medical treatment.

An hour after leaving the attorney's office Bill met with Dr. Small. He found himself talking with Dr. Small like they were old friends.

"Dr. Small, I have an excellent and knowledgeable staff. They know the people and are more than qualified to assist you in their care. I cannot thank you enough for doing this on such short notice," Bill told him.

"Son, I will be happy to help. You just get back here to the people who need you after this war is over," Dr. Small said.

"Thank you. Once I get back home I will speak with everyone about our arrangements."

"I am anxious to meet both of these ladies you think so much of. When do you have to leave?" Dr. Small asked.

"Valentine's Day," Bill told him.

"Son, I know you are in a hurry to get home but I would appreciate it if you would join my family for dinner. My daughter is a nurse and will be leaving Monday. My wife could use a little distraction, if you understand my meaning," Dr. Small said.

Bill stopped and thought for a moment, then made the choice to stay; nothing had gone as he planned since his arrival in Augusta. What would a few more hours matter?

"I would be honored to join you for dinner," Bill said.

CHAPTER TWENTY-ONE

0800, *February 2, 1942*
Augusta, Georgia
Red Cross Office

*S*usan stood with thirty women; right hand raised, and repeated her oath of enlistment. The voices were strong and firm, no whispers as the final words were spoken, "So help me God."

A female officer then escorted all of them to a room, where they were given uniforms.

"Ladies, you have six hours to change clothes, finalize your needs, and meet me at the train station at 1400," the officer told them.

Susan looked around at the small women who stood next to her. She seemed to be confused by the last comment. "Can I help you? My name is Susan."

"Thank you, yes. My name is Nancy Small and what the hell is 1400?" she asked.

Susan laughed; while she worked in Chile during the earthquake she had become familiar with military time. "It's military time, meaning 2:00 p.m."

"Goodness, seems like a mouthful, doesn't it?" Nancy asked her.

"Susan Jane," Henry walked up and hugged his niece. "I am proud of you, girl, but still scared." He wiped away a tear.

"I will be fine, Uncle Henry," Susan responded.

"How much time have you got?" he asked.

"Six hours and then we all meet at the train station," Susan answered.

"Let's go get a bite to eat and then I need to head home."

"I need to change and give you my clothes to take back. We cannot take any of our own with us," Susan told her uncle.

Uncle Henry looked at the small woman who stood next to Susan. "Would you like to join us?"

"Thank you, but I promised my father I would come by the house before I leave. Susan, I will meet you at the train station. You are the only person I have met so far and I would appreciate your company to wherever we are going," Nancy told them.

"I will see you at 1400," Susan said, smiling at her new friend.

❦

9:00 a.m.

ℬill opened the door of his office to a waiting room full of patients. Smiles and friendly greetings met him this morning. He had left Augusta late Saturday night after staying to have dinner with Dr. Small and his family. The drive home had added another wrench into his plans. He had a flat tire and had slept in the car until morning so he could see to change it. Sunday had been a day to recoup and start making preparations to leave. He would talk to Susan this morning and make plans to get married this weekend. He could smell coffee from the back and was anxious to see her. Bill walked to the back quickly and grabbed his white coat.

Angie and Ida heard the door open and his greetings to the folks out front.

"Mom, I can't tell him. You have to do it," Angie told her.

"Angie, life is not always easy. We'll do it together."

Ida and Angie walked to Bill's office where he sat looking at the mail he had received on Friday. He heard footsteps and assumed it was Susan.

"Susan, I need to talk . . . " Bill looked up to see Angie and Ida. "Where's Susan?"

❦

1400

𝒜ugusta Train Station

"Susan, wait up," Nancy ran down the platform in her uniform to where Susan stood.

"Did you get to see your family?" Susan asked.

"My dad is a doctor here in town and we had lunch with Mother at home. Where is your uncle?" Nancy asked.

"I sent him on his way. I am used to traveling alone and there was no need for him to wait."

Susan and Nancy stepped up into the train and found two seats together. They now faced two women wearing the same uniform. They were having a conversation and looked up when Susan and Nancy sat down.

"Hello, my name is Dawn Goodson and this is my friend Pam Lyles. We're from Macon. We have been here for three days waiting to leave."

"I'm Nancy Small and this is Susan . . . oh, dear, I don't know your last name," she said.

"Bowen, Susan Bowen from Waynesboro," she answered.

"It's nice to meet everyone," Pam said.

"Does anyone know where we are going?" Nancy asked.

First Lieutenant Dorothy Freedman heard the conversation as she walked into the middle of the car. "Ladies, I am your commanding officer, First Lieutenant Freedman. We are headed to New York and that is all I am allowed to tell any of you at this time."

There were murmurs throughout the car from the thirty women.

"I suggest you get comfortable, we have a long ride ahead of us."

*B*ill sat in his office after finishing a very long day. He needed a drink but the only thing to drink was cold coffee. He was hurt and disappointed to hear Susan had left without waiting until he returned. There was tension most of the day but Ida's motherly request to come to dinner was the opportunity he needed to give them more bad news. He had sent Ida and Angie home so he could be alone. Bill needed time to figure out why all of this had happened. Time slipped away and he was brought back to the present when Henry called to him.

"Doc, time for dinner," Henry told him.

"Did Ida send you?" Bill asked.

Henry took a deep breath. "No, I just got back from Augusta and thought I had better stop."

"Did she say anything?" Bill asked.

Henry bowed his head for a moment, and then looked up at Bill. "No."

"Ida told me Susan left a letter. I guess I should read it," Bill told Henry.

"Bill, Susan has always been different. The fact that she has stayed around this long surprised all of us. I do know she cares a great deal for you."

"I guess she didn't care enough to stay," Bill said.

The two men left the office and Henry drove them to the house. Bill could smell fried chicken as he got out of the truck.

"Comfort food, for those who need to be comforted," Bill said.

"I can smell apple pie," Henry said and smiled.

The men went inside and took their places at the table. Bill had become so much a part of this family he automatically reached out to join hands for the blessing. There was little conversation during dinner.

Ida looked at the empty plates on the table. "Boys, I want you to clear the table and then go outside. I will call you when I am ready for you to come back."

Bill watched Jacob and Josh do as they were told. They never questioned the fact that adult talk was about to take place and they knew it involved Aunt Susan.

Angie brought coffee to the table. Ida cut pie for those still at the table. She then went to the kitchen and brought back the black box and letter for Bill.

"Susan didn't want it to come to a letter, Bill. She had to leave to make her enlistment and trip out today," Ida told him.

Bill held the box that had meant the hope of love and family for him. He didn't feel this was the appropriate time to read Susan's letter. Bill looked up into faces of the people who he now called family.

"It's funny; we were in Augusta at the same time and never knew it. I have known for some time she was going to join the military," Bill said. He looked into their faces and could see his announcement caught them off guard.

"She only told us a few days ago," Angie told him.

"How long have you known?" Henry asked.

"Since the wedding. She told me at the big house later that night," Bill answered.

"Why didn't you say something to one of us before now?" Ida asked.

"You know Susan, when she makes her mind up it's hard to change it. I thought proposing would make her want to stay. I thought she loved me enough to stay. I was wrong," Bill told them.

"Bill, no one has ever been able to talk, force, or humiliate Susan Jane into doing anything she didn't want. We have all learned that over the years," Ida said.

"Well, this only makes what I have to tell you even more difficult. I have been called back to active military service," Bill said.

"No, please, not you, too," Angie said and put her face into her hands.

"Called back? You have been in the service before?" Henry asked.

"Yes, that was the reason I was gone all of last week. I was basically ordered to Augusta and stuck there filling out papers, tests, a physical . . . it was never-ending," Bill told them.

"When do you have to leave? What about the office?" Ida inquired.

Bill watched as Angie stood and left the table. "I must report to Augusta on the fourteenth, be given my orders for my assignment, and shipped out that day. Ida, I have made arrangements for a Dr. Nathaniel Small to come twice a week and see patients. He is a good man and reasonable when it comes to natural healing. His daughter left today, probably on the same train as Susan."

"We'll do our best while you are gone. You will come back, won't you?" Ida asked as a tear ran down her cheek.

"God willing, maybe Susan will give me another chance," Bill said.

Bill decided there had been enough bad news for one day. He put the box and letter in his coat pocket.

"Ida, thank you for dinner. I need to notify all the patients I see on a regular basis. The last day I will be in the office will be the Wednesday before I have to leave Waynesboro. I am going to pack all my things," Bill said.

"Son, don't pack anything; just leave things where they are, you'll be back. I'll take care of your car, too," Henry told him.

Bill was touched deeply by this family and their continued concern for him. "I am an only child and both my parents are gone. You are the closest thing I have to a real family. If it would be all right with both of you I am going to inform the military you are my next of kin. I had this made while I was in Augusta. I would appreciate you keeping it in a safe place. It's my last will and testament," he handed Ida the envelope.

Ida swallowed hard. "That would be just fine and I will give this back to you the day you return."

"Henry, would you take me to Augusta when it's time?" Bill asked.

"I would be honored," Henry answered.

As Bill walked out, the cold night air hit him in the face. This was the feeling of loneliness. His thoughts of leaving for foreign lands, men injured and dying, and endless hours in surgery were more than he wanted to deal with at this moment. He looked out and saw Angie standing away from the house. He walked up, not sure what to say to her.

"Angie, I am so sorry about all this. I had hoped Susan would marry me, stay here, and be with you when the baby came," Bill told her.

"Bill, I cannot stand any more bad news . . . Jerry, Susan, and now you. How many more of the people I love will the damn war take from me?" Angie asked him. "Unfair, so unfair for all of us."

"Yes, it is," Bill said, and then wrapped his arm around her shoulders and let her cry.

Leland, Mississippi

$\mathscr{D}$ealer looked at the black dress that hung on her door. The memorial service for Uncle Sonny was in the morning at the church. Her uncle's body would be forever entombed with his comrades on the USS Arizona in Hawaii. She would have to be strong for her maw. She could hear her paw locking the front door and knew he would stop by her room before going to bed.

"Deelyn, are you still awake?" Butch asked.

"About to go to bed, Paw," Dealer answered.

"After the service tomorrow we need to go out to the hangar for about an hour."

"Is something wrong?" Dealer asked.

"No, before this memorial was set up I was contacted by a man who wanted to hire a pilot. He said he worked for the military. I set up a meeting tomorrow so he can meet you."

CHAPTER TWENTY-TWO

February 7, 1942
New York City

The cold weather of New York made Larry long to be back in San Francisco. He wished they had been there for more than forty-eight hours so they could have seen more of the beauty of the city on the bay. One day he would return and take the time necessary to explore all that he missed. He was not sure how long he would be home; it could possibly be a month or he and his buddies could be shipped out tomorrow. There had only been time for a short visit with his family and a quick trip to the *Daily*. Today he would introduce his new friends to New York and later they would all go dancing at the USO. He hoped for a good band and a beautiful woman who could dance. In the past he had discovered that beautiful women and dancing didn't always go together. Larry knew this could be the last time he would hold a woman in his arms for a while.

"Hey, Larry, time to go show us bums around," a familiar voice called.

"I'm ready, B.O.," Larry said.

"You son of a bitch. I wish you had never called me that in front of everyone else; now I can't get rid of it," Bernard Orin Woods told his friend.

Larry laughed at him; B.O. was a New Jersey native and a good journalist. They had met in San Francisco when B.O. joined the unit, and they became instant friends.

"Well, you are stuck with it now."

"Bastard," B.O. responded.

Larry finished his notes on the story he started about his introduction to life in the military as a civilian reporter. He reached for his jacket and started to put his cigarettes in the inside pocket but remembered the necklace was there. Larry started to leave it in his room but left it where it had been since he left Hawaii, next to his heart. He left the building along with a dozen other men. He would be their guide to the sights and sounds of the city.

Susan waited for her new friends, Nancy, Dawn, and Pam, now dubbed the "Georgia Peaches." Out of the thirty nurses who arrived in New York they were the only ones who would be leaving Monday morning. They had not been told where they were going but all had been issued enough equipment to build muscles if they carried it very far. The "Georgia Peaches" had been indoctrinated quickly into military life, chain of command, how to salute, and reprimands should they not follow orders. They were given the rank of second lieutenant, officers, and along with rank would come responsibility. Susan questioned her new friends and found that all had similar qualifications. They were skilled in surgery, had requested to be task force nurses, and Nancy had a background in anesthesia. Susan had learned her surgery skills in Chile. She had gone to help and was given a skill that would place her where she would be needed most.

"Susan, you are always early. Can you believe how cold it is here?" Nancy asked.

"Where are Dawn and Pam?" Susan returned the question.

"Here," Dawn said.

"The answer to your question about the weather, Nancy, is no; but at least the army gave us a warm coat," Susan said.

"I am ready to dance and have a drink," Pam said as she did a quick dance step.

"Food first, please. I am starving," Nancy begged.

"Lieutenant Freedman gave me directions to a wonderful Italian restaurant. It's close to the USO," Susan said.

"Let's go. I hear there will be a good dance band playing tonight," Pam told them, and did one more quick dance step to show off.

"I swear she stopped every service man on the way to this building asking about the USO and who was playing," Dawn said.

"Off we go! Food, music, and dancing are on our list for tonight," Susan said.

The "Georgia Peaches" left for their night out in the cold of New York City.

2000
USO

*L*arry had treated his friends to the best of New York. The group now walked toward the USO. All branches of the service were seen on the streets, including the military police. Their presence made sure soldiers behaved or felt the consequences. He could hear the band playing and was ready to dance. The door opened to a sea of men and women in uniforms. Larry found a corner while his buddies went in twelve different directions. He took a cigarette out and lit it. A few minutes later B.O. came back with a sandwich stuffed in his mouth.

"Larry, you need to see all the food they have in the next room," B.O. told him, and pointed across to the other side of the dance floor.

"Jesus, how can you possibly have any room after the meal we had tonight?" Larry asked.

"I can always eat," B.O. answered.

Larry laughed and then looked at the front door as four women walked inside together. They took their coats off and he could see they were army. The band began to play "Oh! Look at Me Now," by Tommy Dorsey.

"*I* am glad to get in here," Pam said.

"Me, too, that was a little longer walk than I wanted in the cold, even with our coats," Nancy said.

"I see empty tables, ladies," Dawn told them.

Susan and her friends began to make their way toward the other side of the dance floor.

"Can you believe all the men in here?" Pam asked incredulously. Her three friends stopped, turned, and looked at her.

"What?" Pam asked.

"I am ashamed to be your friend," Dawn answered

Larry looked up as the four passed by him. The woman in the lead turned, looked directly into his eyes, and then smiled as if she knew him. A chill ran down his back and a familiar scent surrounded him. Lilacs. His heart began to race and his hands shook. Larry looked at his friend.

"Do you smell that?" Larry asked B.O.

"Smell what? All I can smell is your cigarette and this corned beef," B.O. answered.

"You can't smell the lilacs?"

"Lilacs? Are you crazy? There are so many women in here, how can you possibly pick one fragrance out over another?" B.O. asked.

Larry didn't hear B.O.'s last comment. He headed toward the blonde who seemed to see into his very soul and carried the scent of the woman who saved his life at Pearl Harbor.

Susan's friends noticed the odd exchange between the stranger and their friend. Nancy reached up and tapped her friend on the shoulder.

"Susan, do you know that man?" Nancy asked.

"What man?" Susan responded.

"Are you kidding? The man you almost stared a hole through," Dawn told her.

"I don't know what you are talking about. Why?" Susan said.

"Because the man you didn't stare at is following you," Pam said.

Susan stopped, turned around to see what her friends were talking about, and looked up into the greenest eyes she had ever seen. For a moment she thought she knew the man who stood before her.

*L*arry was taken by surprise when she turned around and looked up at him. She had the same beautiful blue eyes he had seen at Pearl.

"Would you like to dance?" Larry asked, but didn't allow an answer. He took her hand, gave her coat to one of the other women, and pulled her out to the dance floor.

"We'll save you a seat," Nancy screamed as this stranger took her friend away.

"I didn't know Susan knew anyone in New York," Pam said.

"She doesn't," Nancy answered.

"It sure looks like she knows him," Dawn told them.

Larry took this woman who didn't have a name to the dance floor. The band began to play "At Last," by Glen Miller. He took her into his arms.

"I am sorry, my name is Larry White," he said.

"Susan. And it's quite all right," she answered.

The two said nothing else while the music played. For a moment in time, two hearts and souls who had been lost seemed to have found one another.

*O*nce the song ended, Larry walked Susan to where her friends sat. He watched as his buddies found him and the four beautiful women. The "Georgia Peaches" were popular for the rest of the night. They danced and laughed until the final song, "Be Careful, it's in My Heart," by Bing Crosby, started playing.

"Susan, are you and Larry going to . . . " Nancy started to ask.

"You're late with your question," B.O. told her and pointed to the dance floor.

"Larry, I have had a wonderful evening," Susan told him.

"Would it be possible for me to see you tomorrow?" Larry asked.

"We have an early morning meeting but I will be free after 1300," Susan answered.

"Where can I meet you?"

"We are staying in some apartments above the *White Daily Journal.* Do you need directions?" Susan asked.

"I think I can find it," Larry said and smiled.

"Time to go, Susan," Pam called to Susan.

"Do you ladies need an escort home?" B.O. asked.

"No, the MP's made arrangements for us to be escorted, but thanks," Nancy told him.

Larry escorted Susan and the others to the front door of the USO. "See you tomorrow, Susan." Larry said. Before he could stop or think Larry took Susan in his arms and kissed her.

"Tomorrow," Susan said and walked away with her friends.

The "Georgia Peaches" left with their MP escort.

"Damn it, girl, you have got some explaining to do when we get home tonight," Pam told her.

"Regardless, I say get him before another woman comes along," Dawn said, smiled, and lit a cigarette.

Susan looked at Nancy and they smiled at each other. Susan could still feel the heat in her face and the touch of his lips on hers.

L arry and his buddies headed back to their accommodations. B.O. walked up next to his friend.

"I thought you didn't know her," B.O. said.

"I don't," Larry answered.

"Are you sure?"

Larry turned around and watched the car Susan was in disappear from his sight.

"Well, not in this lifetime anyway," Larry answered, and then walked off.

Sunday, 1200
White Daily Journal

L arry had a restless night, little sleep, and a need to see Susan again. He decided to stop in the office to see his brother before meeting her. He tried to decide if an apology was in order or another kiss when he saw her. He looked up and saw his brother waving his arms frantically at him as he entered the front door.

"Lawrence, you are not going to believe this. I can't believe it," Emmitt told him.

"Well, hello to you too, brother," Larry said.

"I have something for you, a letter from a beautiful woman. She and three others had been staying in the apartments upstairs."

Larry did not have a good feeling about the letter Emmitt had for him.

"You are not going to believe who she is; I couldn't believe who she was . . . is. She was so close and I just didn't know," Emmitt was rambling.

"Emmitt, what are you talking about?" Larry asked.

"Here, read this and I'll tell you."

Larry,

I am asking for a rain check on our afternoon. The meeting this morning was our immediate orders to leave. By the time you read this I will have been gone for several hours. This kind man said he knew you and would give this letter to you. I am breaking the rules but we are headed to England.

Any chance you will wait for me?

Susan

Larry was upset and a little uneasy they had been shipped out so quickly, but this could have happened to him at any moment.

"Are you done?" Emmitt asked.

"Okay, now what is so important about this woman? This letter has ruined what I had hoped would have been a great afternoon," Larry responded.

"Her last name."

"Emmitt, I swear you sound like Grandfather the last time I saw him," Larry told him.

"It's Bowen; the woman who left this letter is the family we are trying to find for the trust."

Larry stood for a moment and looked at his brother. "Are you sure?"

"Yes, when she was leaving I asked for her name. She was in a hurry and turned at the door. *My name is Susan Bowen, from Waynesboro, Georgia.* Before I could stop her they were in a taxi and gone."

CHAPTER TWENTY-THREE

0700, April 15, 1942
Leland, Mississippi

*D*avid Fines, operational advisor for the military, sat in his car and waited for Dealer to finish her preflight check. Two months ago when he was introduced to this pilot he had been skeptical about her abilities. Dealer had proved herself many times as an experienced pilot and someone who could be counted on. This Mississippi sprite had earned his respect with each flight they completed. He checked his paperwork and clearances for the bases they would fly into this week. The background check on Dealer and her family was swift and positive. He never had a question about her or the family's loyalty to their country. David had been called on by his country to help after Pearl Harbor. He had retired from the military after forty years of service. He accepted the request from two old friends for his assistance and knowledge, friends who now carried the same stars on their shoulders that he once wore.

Dealer walked up to David's car and knocked on the window. "Mr. Fines, I am ready to go."

David and Dealer made their way into the plane and he handed her their destination for the next day or two.

"We're going to Texas?" Dealer asked.

"Yes, Waco, Victoria, San Antonio, and maybe one more. Do you have an overnight bag with you?" David asked her.

"Always," Dealer answered, and then started the plane and taxied out to the runway.

"I received the clearances necessary for you to land on the bases. No more civilian airfields," David told her.

Dealer smiled.

South Pacific
Evacuation Unit

*B*ill sat down in the mess tent for a cup of coffee and a moment alone. He knew he should eat but his appetite had disappeared as of late and that could be one reason his uniform now seemed looser. He had been in surgery for the last eighteen hours and all he wanted was a shower and his cot. His thoughts slipped away to Georgia and a walk with Susan on a cool Easter Sunday afternoon. He remembered how beautiful she was that day and the glimmer of red in her blonde hair. Bill had received letters from Ida and one from Angie. They both spoke highly of Dr. Small. The people of Waynesboro sent their love and awaited his return. He reached in his pocket and pulled out a folded envelope that held the letter he had yet to read. *No time like the present*, he thought. Bill had put this off long enough. He took the letter out and unfolded the paper.

> *Bill,*
>
> *This is not the way I intended to answer your proposal. You have left me no choice but to write a letter. I wish you were here so we could talk face to face.*
>
> *Please believe me when I tell you I never meant for emotions and feelings to evolve as they did for you. I have always been a wandering spirit and never meant to hurt you. I will not insult you with excuses, but simply say I cannot marry you. I will ask you to watch over Angie and the good folk of Waynesboro; they need you.*
>
> *Please don't wait for me.*
>
> *Susan*

Bill stood, leaving the odor of food he did not want and voices he no longer wished to hear. He walked up to the fire barrel outside the tent he shared with other surgeons. It was a sad attempt to keep the pests away that fed on everyone in the camp. He took the letter, lit the end, and watched as it and a life he had hoped for turned to ash.

Waco, Texas
Airbase

"*Dealer*, you can come inside once the plane has been refueled," David told her.

"Yes, sir, I'll do that," Dealer answered.

She waited until he was out of sight and made a straight line for the planes that sat inside a hangar. Dealer made a quick assessment and found she was alone. She walked over to the Valiant and the Texan. Dealer knew these were trainers. She took a glove off and ran her hand down the side of the Texan. *Who will know?* she thought, and then walked up to the left side of the plane and stepped up.

David's meeting this morning was his introduction to the commanding officer of the base and schedule comparisons for the next few months. He looked at his watch and knew he and Dealer needed to leave so they could make the next meeting. He entered the hallway and was met by two MPs who called him by name.

"General Fines, sir, do you have a civilian pilot on the base?" the soldier asked.

"Yes, I do, gentlemen. Is there a problem?" David replied.

"Sir, could you come with us?"

David was not sure what Dealer had done but it could not be good if the MPs were asking about her.

As David and the MPs entered the hangar he stifled a laugh at the sight of Dealer's feet sticking out of the cockpit. It had to be the funniest thing he had ever seen.

Dealer had been so fascinated with the Texan she had lost all thought of time. She was bent over the cockpit of the plane, about to reach for a log book that lay on the seat, when she heard someone clear his voice. Dealer looked under her arm to see to the military police and Mr. Fines.

"Ma'am, would you come down from there please?" the MP asked her.

Dealer backed her way out of the cockpit, straightened her jacket, and made her way off the plane.

"*S*ir, do you know this woman?" the MP asked.

"Yes, this is my pilot," David answered. He walked over, handed Dealer his handkerchief, and pointed to her nose.

"It would be advisable for her to be instructed on the areas civilians are allowed, sir," he said.

"I will take care of it, thank you," David said.

The MPs walked away.

"I'm sorry, it's just I haven't had a chance to get this close and I didn't mean to get you in trouble. I am really sorry," Dealer told him.

"I am not the one who was found head deep in a place reserved for uniformed personnel. In the future, I would appreciate you not taking any more unscheduled excursions," David said.

"You're not going to fire me?" Dealer asked.

"Not at the moment," David answered.

He wished his sons had half the daring this young woman exhibited. David thought about the one thing Dealer did not tell him and that was that she would not do it again. He knew this would not be the first or last time Dealer would be found in restricted areas. He chuckled as he followed her back to the plane and headed for Victoria. David decided he would make a stop at the MP offices in the future. They should be informed about his spirited young pilot and her wandering curiosity when it came to planes.

Ireland

*J*acqueline Antoinette Monfaire, or Jam, as her American friends called her, sat smoking a cigarette in her tent and read the news from home. Jam was a reporter for a Canadian newspaper and had fought her way into this war. She had the right to be here and report just like her male counterparts. At least this was the story she told anyone who would listen. The sound of footsteps caused her to stop reading and look up at the stranger who passed by.

"Qui est ce?" Jam asked.

Patricia Hentone looked at her tall friend. "English. Damn it, Jam. We need to speak English."

*P*at was Jam's photographer and the two complemented each other well. Pat thought about their political beliefs that drew them together in college. The war now gave them the opportunity they needed to participate in those beliefs. Jam's family was wealthy and they doted on their only child, too much Pat thought. Due to the Monfaire wealth both women had been given preferential treatment, background checks forgone, and both women slipped through without question or suspect. Pat remembered painfully her attempt to learn the French language not once but twice, and failed both times, miserably. She thought about her French instructor cursing; at least she thought it was cursing. It was in French so she never knew for sure. Unable to speak French almost kept her from making this trip until Pat explained she was fluent in German.

"You should be ashamed, mon ami," Jam told her.

"Okay, I know that means my friend, but what else did you say?" Pat asked.

"I said I need to meet that tall man," Jam told her.

"I don't think so, but I am too tired to argue with you, bitch," Pat answered.

*J*am watched her small friend curl up like a cat on her cot to take a nap. She had to find the handsome man who walked by and become acquainted. It had been too long since her sexual appetite had been satisfied. Jam stood and quickly brushed her long brown hair and tied it back with a red ribbon. She looked into a small mirror.

"A la recherché de l'amour infinit, c'est que, un peu difficile, ah merde," Jam said. Love, sweet love.

Jam followed her instinct and went to the mess tent. The tall man who walked past her tent sat alone reading a letter. She obtained two cups of coffee and turned and walked toward him. Jam intended to introduce him to an international relationship.

 arry had settled into a routine over the last few days since arriving in Ireland. He could not believe the beauty of the countryside. He followed the smell of coffee and decided to read the letters from home he had received yesterday at mail call. Larry had attempted to find where Susan and her friends had been sent. His investigative practices paid off and he sent a letter to her APO address. God knew when she would receive it. Larry had begun to read a letter from his mother when he heard French.

"Bonjour, bel homme charmant," a female voice said.

Larry looked up and took the coffee that had been handed to him. "Thank you for that compliment. Would you like to sit down?"

"You speak French?" she asked.

"French, Italian, and some Spanish," Larry told her.

"My name is Jam. I am impressed and now intrigued. Tell me about yourself and how you ended up here in this tent with me." She then reached out and ran her finger across the back of his hand.

Larry had an uncanny ability to read people. He felt this woman was trouble and needed an excuse to leave the tent.

B.O. had walked into the tent and observed Larry and the Canadian doll he had seen when they arrived. "Bastard gets all the women," he said out loud, then headed straight for his buddy.

Larry saw B.O. when he entered the tent and decided to use him for an excuse to leave.

"Larry, who is . . . " B.O. started.

"B.O., damn it, man, I know we are going to be late for that meeting. Sorry, Jam, if you will excuse me, we have to leave. It's been a pleasure. Maybe I will see you around," Larry said.

B.O. didn't know what the hell he was talking about, but went along. "Yeah, man, we need to go now."

Larry stood and grabbed B.O. by the arm, all but dragging him out of the tent, leaving Jam at the table.

"What the hell are you doing?" B.O. asked.

"Saving my life I'm pretty sure," Larry answered.

"Well do me a favor and don't save me if I ever get to talk to her," B.O. replied.

Jam watched Larry and his buddy leave the tent. "Et voila, je suis patiente je peux attendre. I'll be waiting," Jam said.

England

    Susan and Nancy had been given permission to go into town for the afternoon. Their training since they arrived had been intense and fast paced. Any time that was given to them was cherished and not wasted. Their friends were on duty but had given a list of personal items to bring back. Tomorrow would be busy for all of them. They were being sent to Ireland for a surgical conference to improve their skills in the field. Today was a treat to have a few hours away from work. Susan obtained a Jeep from the motor pool and both women bounced as Susan hit a bump in the road as they headed to town.

"Susan, where are we going in such a hurry?" Nancy asked.

"The Culpeper house," Susan answered.

"Again, weren't you there just a week ago?"

"Yes, this is a treasure for me. So many herbs and oils. I can make some soaps, creams, and teas," Susan said.

"I never knew there were so many uses for herbs until I met you," Nancy said, then laughed.

"Nature provides everything we need if you know how to use it. My family has used herbs for more than a hundred years. We have a school in Waynesboro to teach the proper use, cultivation, and storage for preservation."

"Waynesboro, that's what I wanted to ask you about," Nancy told her.

"Can it wait until after we leave the shop? We can stop down the street and have tea and cake?" Susan asked.

"That'll be fine," Nancy said.

Susan found a safe place to park the Jeep and gave a boy who looked about twelve years old some money to watch it. They walked down the street and entered the Culpeper house. Susan quickly picked out all the items she needed. She found a book with information on herbs and plants of Europe. This book could be of use once they left England. Susan made her purchases and the two left the shop. Once they left the Culpeper house it was time for tea. Susan knew Nancy loved the place they were headed. They sat down in a corner table close to the window.

"Do you miss your home, Susan?" Nancy asked.

"Sometimes, but I miss my cousin Angie more. She is about six months pregnant now and I would love to see a picture of her," Susan said and took the tea and cakes from the lady who came to the table. The owner knew them from their previous times there and had brought their usual requests.

"I am an only child. I told you my father was a physician, didn't I?" Nancy asked.

"Yes, I remember you telling me the day we left Augusta," Susan answered.

"Did I tell you about the physician who had dinner with my family the Saturday night before we left?"

"No, why is it important?" Susan asked.

"Well, the only reason I'm mentioning it is because he was from Waynesboro," Nancy responded.

Susan stopped and looked at Nancy. "His name wasn't Bill Benjamin, was it?"

"Yes, do you know him?"

"Bill is the local physician in Waynesboro. We are lucky to have him there. My cousin and I work for him; at least I did until I enlisted," Susan told her friend. She could not imagine what Bill was doing at her house having dinner.

"Is he married?" Nancy asked.

"No, why are you asking?"

"I was just curious. Hopefully he won't find someone while he is gone and get married. I think he is a very handsome man," Nancy told Susan.

"What do you mean while he's gone? Bill is in Waynesboro taking care of the patients and watching over my cousin," Susan said.

"You don't know?" Nancy asked.

Susan picked up her cup of tea. "Know what, Nancy?"

"Dr. Benjamin was called back into military service. My father made an agreement to take care of his patients until he returns from the war," Nancy answered.

Susan dropped her cup on the shop floor, spilling her tea and shattering the small cup.

Nancy stood up to see if Susan was hurt. "Susan, are you all right, did you burn yourself?" Nancy asked, then looked at her friend and saw the tears running down her face. "Susan, what's wrong? Are you all right?"

Susan regained her composure and looked at her friend. She could see the worry in Nancy's face. "Nancy, did he say where he was going?" Susan asked.

"No, just that he would be shipped out on Valentine's Day. Susan, was there something between you and Dr. Benjamin?" Nancy asked. She knew her friend's reaction was not without reason.

The shop owner came, cleaned up the broken cup, and brought Susan another cup of tea. Susan thanked the lady and offered to pay for the cup. The shop owner just put her hand on Susan's shoulder, smiled, and shook her head no.

Susan was not sure how much she should reveal to Nancy. She now understood the rush to get married, Bill's sudden trip, all the delays home from Augusta. It all made sense. She knew Bill would never leave just anyone to watch over Angie or the good folks back home. He was a good man.

"Nancy, I allowed something to happen and then did not take appropriate measures to stop it. Now he is God knows where with a letter. What does that say about me?" Susan told her.

"I'm sorry for the both of you," Nancy said, then reached out and squeezed Susan's hand.

"That's what my cousin said. I guess it's time I sit down and read the letters from home," Susan told her.

Susan and Nancy filled the requests they had been given and returned to their quarters. Susan ran in and dropped her purchases on her bed and began to rummage through her things, looking for letters from home.

"Well, it's good to see you two back. It was busy in surgery today. I am beat," Pam told them.

"Anything good in town?" Dawn asked.

"Only if you like the Culpeper house," Nancy answered.

"Have you two seen my letters? I thought I put them in . . . there they are," Susan said.

"You got another one today. Let me get it for you," Pam told Susan.

"I can't believe you went back to that shop again!" Dawn said.

"I didn't hear you complain when she made that—what was it?" Pam asked.

"Poultice, it's called a poultice," Nancy answered.

"Yeah, that poultice which helped your bruised back during training," Pam told Dawn.

"Is it another letter from home?" Susan asked.

"I don't think so; the name on the return is White," Pam answered.

"White, isn't that the name of your dance partner in New York?" Dawn teased.

Susan stopped looking at letters from home and walked over and took the letter out of Pam's hand. Pam was right; it was from the man she stood up, the one who had kissed her, the one she asked to wait for her.

"Susan, your letters from home. You need to read them first. Angie, your aunt, remember?" Nancy reminded Susan.

"I will, Nancy, I promise," Susan answered.

Susan sat down on her bed and took the letters and made the decision to do what was right instead of ripping open the letter from Larry White.

"Susan, we're going to eat. Do you want to go?" Nancy asked.

"No, you go on with Pam and Dawn. I need . . . I have to take time and read these letters and try to find out what is going on at home," Susan told her.

"We'll be back after chow," Pam said.

Susan didn't hear them as they left. She had opened one letter from Angie that held a photograph of her pregnant cousin. The radio played "Careless," by Glenn Miller, as she began to read about family and hopefully that they had heard from Bill. She remembered how Nancy had talked about him at tea and smiled. Over the next hour she read letters from her family in Waynesboro and from her sisters who now lived outside of Houston so they could be closer to their husbands. Both men were stationed in Galveston. Susan's baby sister had heard from Frank, their brother. He had joined the air force more than a year ago, long before Pearl Harbor. She didn't have much information except he was stationed somewhere in Texas. Angie's letters were emotional, her worries over Jerry and his dwindling letters that were censored by the government. She wrote about Dr. Small and his kindness to her and Aunt Ida. Angie said, *I feel safe about my care and the baby's after working with Dr. Small. Bill made a good choice.* There was no comment of Bill's reaction to the return of the ring or letter.

The last letter Susan opened was from Aunt Ida. It contained similar information about Waynesboro and Dr. Small, her work collecting metal, rubber, the rationing, and that they were better off than many in the community. Aunt Ida said she had received one letter from Bill. He couldn't tell her where he was, only that malaria was the enemy. Susan closed her eyes; he was in the South Pacific where heavy fighting had taken place. Aunt Ida finished the letter reminding Susan to say her prayers and to write. Susan looked at the letters on the bed and cried. She had been careless and thoughtless of the people who loved and cared for her. *How could the dead be proud of her when she had ignored the living?*

Susan would write and send pictures of the "Georgia Peaches" to her family in the next few days. She would do better . . . she had to do better.

Susan looked up to see her friends had returned.

"Damn, I hope those letters had a little good news in them. You look as though the world is about to end," Dawn said.

"They are filled with reminders of a family that loves and cares about me. I have become selfish and irresponsible of their feelings," Susan responded and wiped her face.

"What about the letter from Mr. White?" Pam asked.

"I will read it tomorrow; tonight my family comes first," Susan told her.

Nancy smiled and handed Susan a sandwich she had made for her. "Susan, I don't think your family would mind if you read one

more letter as long as theirs are the ones you answer first."

"C'mon, don't you want to know about the man from New York?" Pam asked.

Susan looked at the vultures that hovered around her bed, waiting. "All right, let's see what he has to say."

A cheer went up as Susan opened the letter and began to read through her red and swollen eyes.

CHAPTER TWENTY-FOUR

April 19, 1942

"*H*urry up, Susan, the train leaves in twenty minutes," Dawn yelled.

Susan had finished her letters to family. She apologized for not writing sooner and promised to do better in the months to come. The last thing to do was mail them, along with a short note to Larry. His letter had been sweet and he apologized for the kiss. He asked Susan to keep in contact along with the promise to meet in New York for a proper dinner after the war. The "Georgia Peaches" were on their way to Ireland for a three-day conference on surgical procedures in the field.

"Back in a jiffy," Susan told her friends as she walked in to post her letters.

"I cannot wait to see a castle," Nancy said.

"What? The ones here aren't enough for you?" Pam asked.

"It's the difference in architecture and masonry," Nancy tried to explain.

"Whoa, that's above my pay grade. They're old and that's good enough for me," Pam said.

Susan could hear the laughter of her friends as she returned to the Jeep. "What did I miss?"

"Oh nothing, just Nancy's history lesson on castles," Dawn said.

"Sounds interesting. Let's go, we don't want to miss the train," Susan told them.

"I brought my new camera just in case we have some free time," Nancy said, and showed them her new prize.

"Is that a Brownie Special?" Pam asked.

"Yes, I got it a few days ago. My father sent it. The package took forever to get here and he sent several rolls of film, too." Nancy was excited.

"Well let's hope we have more than castles to take pictures of . . . like some good-looking men with their arms around us," Dawn said, and leaned over and smiled at the young man who was their driver.

"That will be worth the cost of development," Pam added.

The "Georgia Peaches" laughed as the young private drove out of camp and headed toward the train station.

"B.O., you need to help me out here. Jam shows up everywhere I go lately," Larry told his friend.

"I wish I was so lucky," B.O. answered.

"No, you don't understand. There is this tension between us and she keeps pushing each time I see her."

"Bastard . . . bastard! Why do you get all the women?" B.O. asked.

"This is one I don't want. I caught that friend of hers, Pat, taking my picture coming out of the latrine the other day," Larry told him. He lit a cigarette and looked out the tent flap. Larry had made arrangements for the two of them to ride into town to pick up nurses for the conference. He had to get away from Jam for a few hours so he didn't care what the purpose of the trip was.

"B.O., will you look outside and see if it's clear? We need to leave," Larry said.

"This is nuts, just tell the dame you aren't interested," B.O. said.

"I don't think she is the type to care whether I am interested or not," Larry told him, and then grabbed his coat and another pack of cigarettes. "Let's go."

The two men made it to the transport truck. Larry walked up to the driver's window to tell him they would be in the back. Larry moved up on the step and came face to face with Jam and her friend Pat.

"Mon cher, what are you doing here?" Jam asked and began to laugh.

Larry heard footsteps behind him and turned to see the driver. "We'll be in the back."

The driver acknowledged and crawled into the front seat where Jam preceded to hand him two packages of cigarettes.

"Merci," Jam said.

"Any time, doll," he responded.

Larry crawled into the back of the truck with B.O. and shook his head.

"She found us," Larry told him.

"What?" B.O. said

"She and that friend of hers are sitting in the cab of the truck."

"Man, you are going to have to say or do something," B.O. told Larry.

"My hope is that she will be sent out early with troops going the opposite direction we do."

"Well that would be an easy answer but what if she isn't shipped out early?" B.O. asked.

"Then I will make sure I am sent where she will not want to go," Larry said.

"And where is that?" B.O. inquired.

"Hell."

B.O. looked at his friend. "Never been there; guess I'll go, too."

Larry laughed as the truck bounced its way out of camp.

*S*usan was happy to see the beauty of the countryside. She had worried there would be nothing but devastation, but much had remained unspoiled. She looked around at all the soldiers and the different uniforms; it was confusing. But leave it to her friends to sort out the differences and obtain a few names and addresses along the way.

"This is your station," one of the men announced to Pam.

"Really? So sad to leave, but duty calls," Pam responded.

"It's been nice, too," the soldier said and kissed her cheek.

The four women left the train and watched as the men on board waved goodbye to them.

"You know I am beginning to enjoy my tour of duty each day," Pam said.

"I think we need to meet out front. Someone is supposed to pick us up," Nancy announced.

"God in Heaven, not another bumpy ride," Dawn said and rubbed her bottom.

As the four made their way out front to wait for their ride they joined about twenty women gathered together. Susan walked over and inquired as to their destination and purpose; it was the same as theirs. She motioned to her friends.

"We are all going to the same place," Susan told them.

𝒜 few minutes later the transport truck pulled up to the station. Jam was glad. She needed to stretch her long legs and spend a few private moments with Larry. Jam needed to keep the tension intensifying and not let up. He would eventually give in to her.

"Jam, look at all the women," Pat said.

"They're here for a three-day training course, something to do with surgery in the field," Jam informed her friend.

"They may have more information than we are able to obtain at camp. I'll mingle and see if I can find where they've traveled from and their units," Pat said and took out her camera. She opened the door, got out of the truck, and began to take pictures, which included several of the "Georgia Peaches."

Jam was not interested in the nurses at the moment. She only cared about what rode in the back. She walked around to find Larry. They would go for a long walk; she would kiss and touch him, then leave him wanting as they returned back to camp. Jam smiled and started to call for him when she discovered the back of the truck was empty.

"Mais, pour l'amour, ou sont-ils tous dispare?" Jam said.

Pat heard her friend and walked to the back of the truck.

"Damn it, Jam! English, for the last time, speak English!" Pat said, and then looked into the back of an empty truck. "What the hell?"

Pat turned and looked at her friend.

$\mathcal{L}$arry knew what would happen once the truck stopped. Jam would follow him, interrupt any conversation he tried to have, and move her body into his. Her teasing would appear to be playful to anyone who did not know her or hadn't been the center of her desire. He and B.O. got out at the last checkpoint and waited until the truck was out of sight. He pretended to interview the men at the checkpoint and offered to mail letters home for them to cover their escape. Thirty minutes later they were on their way to town via Jeep.

"How do you think of these things, Larry?" B.O. asked.

"Survival instinct," Larry answered.

"I would love to have seen her face when she found the back empty," B.O. said and laughed.

Larry was not accustomed to being pursued when it came to women. He should be honored but there was something not quite right about Jam. She was not what she presented; there was something that didn't add up. He was usually good at figuring people out but not this time. She was adept at hiding what did not need to be known or questioned; instead she pushed her sexuality.

"I don't believe it," B.O. said as they rode up to the train station.

Larry looked up to see about thirty nurses. He couldn't understand what his comment meant. "What don't you believe? You knew we were coming to pick up nurses."

"Yeah, but did you think we would be picking up the 'Georgia Peaches'?" B.O. asked.

Larry looked up to see Susan and her friends. He jumped out of the Jeep and made his way quickly to where Susan stood. He could not believe she was here.

Nancy saw him first. "Larry? Susan, its Larry White."

Larry walked up and took Susan's arm and kissed her then whispered in her ear, "Yes, I'll wait, I'll wait for you." He smiled as Susan's face began to turn a lovely shade of red.

"Well hello to you, too," Pam said.

"Hello ladies," B.O. said.

"Well this is going to be an interesting conference," Dawn said.

Nancy smiled then looked behind Susan to see two women who had walked around from the back of the transport truck. The tall woman with long hair did not look happy.

Pam looked at Nancy and could see her staring off. "What's wrong?"

"I am not sure," Nancy responded. She took her Brownie and snapped a picture of the two women.

"Why did you do that?"

"Something doesn't seem right," Nancy said.

*J*am's anger increased as she watched the scene unfold before her. Jam had always gotten what she went after and she would deal severely with anyone who got in her way.

"I guess they know each other," Pat said.

"She will only be here for three days. I have the entire war. I can wait. See if you can find out who they are," Jam told Pat.

"Why? Like you said, they will be gone in a few days."

"Just curious," Jam said.

Jam looked at her friend and knew Pat was aware there was more to this than just curiosity. "What's going on with you, Jam?" Pat asked.

"I don't like to lose," Jam answered.

*L*arry's frustration grew over the next few days at the conference. What he had hoped would be time with her had turned into hours of lecture and observation, which left no time for Susan to talk with him. On the third day, at 1900, Larry waited outside the building where the nurses had been cloistered. He knew they would be leaving tomorrow and he had to see her, talk to her, and be with her, if only for an hour. Larry had noticed Jam's absence since the conference started, for which he was grateful but curious. He finished his cigarette when the doors opened and there was an explosion of female voices all talking at the same time. He could see Susan and her friends and started toward them.

"Susan, you have company," Nancy said and smiled at her friend.

"It's too bad you haven't had time to really see him," Pam told her.

"We have a reason for being here. Relationships weren't on the program," Susan said.

"Well he looks like a man on a mission," Dawn told her.

"I'll see you later," Susan said.

"We won't wait up, just don't miss the truck in the morning," Pam yelled.

Susan turned and made a face at her friends.

"What's wrong, Nancy?" Dawn asked.

"I am looking for that tall female reporter. You remember the one at the train station. She has been following us around the camp. She sat in on the conference the first day but I think she was more interested in Susan than the class," Nancy said.

"She is probably just writing a story."

"Maybe," Nancy said.

"What, you think she is a spy?" Dawn said and laughed.

"I don't know what she is," Nancy answered.

Larry knew this may be the only chance he would have to talk with Susan. He had to tell her who he was and what that meant to her family. The trust could be started as soon as he had information from her, but he couldn't get over the feeling he had to be with her.

Larry walked up and kissed Susan on the cheek. "What was that all about?"

"Nothing that would interest you, and stop that or I'm going to get into trouble," Susan told him.

"I really need to talk to you," Larry said.

"Well let's see, if we can find a place where we can hear each other," Susan responded.

"I have a place in mind," Larry said and took her hand, walked to the motor pool, and found the truck where B.O. stood guard.

"The coast is clear. I will be close," B.O. told Larry.

"And this is?" Susan asked.

"The best I could do on short notice," Larry responded.

Larry helped Susan into the back where there was a lantern, table, and dinner waiting.

"How did you pull this off?" Susan asked.

"I have a few friends," Larry smiled.

"And the guard outside?"

"I just want a little privacy and no interruptions," Larry said, then opened a bottle of wine and served dinner.

"I don't even want to know where or how you were able to find wine," Susan told him and laughed.

"Susan, do you remember the place you and your friends were living in New York?" Larry asked.

"Above the newspaper and that kind man I left the letter with for you? Yes, we loved it there," Susan answered and began her meal.

"Emmitt is my older brother and a major pain in the ass. Our family owns the property there in New York," Larry told her.

"Really? They own the building?" Susan asked.

"We own the building, the newspaper, and the trust fund that belongs to your family," Larry announced.

Susan looked up into his green eyes and could not believe who this man was that sat across from her. "Samuel White was your relative?"

"Yes, the man who was in love with your aunt during the civil war," Larry answered.

"How can this be? How is it possible we found one another?" Susan told him.

"Fate," Larry said, and then tipped his glass of wine to Susan.

The next few hours were filled with family ancestry, exchanges of important information for the trust, plans for the future, and a stolen kiss from time to time. Susan had so much more to tell him, but she looked at her watch and it was already 0030.

"Larry, I have to go. The transport leaves at 0700. I don't want to leave but I must," Susan told him.

"Susan, I will send a telegram to my brother to contact your family and have the trust fund money restarted as soon as possible,"

Larry said.

"Thank you. I have something you will want to read."

"What would that be?" Larry asked.

"My aunt's journal she kept during the Civil War while she traveled with other nurses. Did you know your uncle and my aunt were childhood friends?" Susan asked him.

Larry looked at her eyes as they sparkled in the light of the lantern. Was it possible he was falling in love with this woman? Someone he barely knew? He had heard of past lives; could this be one of those moments? *Larry, get a hold of yourself,* the more sensible part of him said.

"I would like to read that one day, and no I didn't know that about him. There seems to be a lot I don't know about my family history," Larry told her. "When this war is over and we are having dinner together in New York we can talk more about the journal. Then I'll hold you in my arms until the sun rises and we'll have champagne served to us in bed." Larry thought about the necklace and how he would give it to her once the war ended and they were safely back home.

Susan stood to leave as Larry pulled back the flap on the truck. B.O. had been good on his word to guard the truck and watch for Jam and her evil twin, Pat. B.O. helped Susan out of the truck.

Larry looked around and stepped down where Susan stood waiting. He walked over, took her in his arms, and kissed her passionately. B.O. turned away.

"I will not apologize for that one. I don't want you to go," Larry said, and held her tightly.

"The war won't last forever. I'll wait for you," Susan said, and touched his face gently.

"I'll walk you to your quarters," Larry said, and nodded to B.O.

B.O. watched as his buddy and Susan left the only privacy they could find. He looked around and began to clear the truck. He would drop the extra packages of smokes to his buddy in the motor pool tomorrow.

*J*am watched through a pair of binoculars as Larry and Susan left.

"Enjoy his company while you can, bitch. Tomorrow is another day and you won't be here to interfere," Jam said.

0700

*L*arry had not slept after taking Susan to her quarters. The same feelings had surfaced again like those in New York. He was uneasy and could not wait to see Susan before she left. Larry and B.O. ate breakfast with the "Georgia Peaches" and then walked them to the transport waiting to leave.

"I'll write, I promise," Susan told him.

"I will hold you to that; we have a date in New York waiting for us," Larry reminded her.

The driver checked to make sure the women were all on board. He secured the back.

Susan leaned down and kissed Larry. "I don't care if I do get in trouble," she said, then touched his face.

Larry looked at her. "I have a surprise for you but it will have to keep until the war is over. Keep your word and wait for me."

Smoke billowed from the pipes of the diesel engine starting. Larry stood and watched the truck bounce down the road. He remained until he could no longer see the truck or Susan's face. He reached inside his pocket and took out the necklace. *Maybe history does repeat itself after all,* he thought, and then replaced it to safety.

Jam waited until the truck was out of sight and made her move to where Larry stood. She wrapped her arm through his and leaned into him. "I am glad all those bitches are gone. What about you?"

Larry took her arm off his, and then turned and faced Jam. She moved into him and tried to wrap her arms around his neck.

Larry caught both her arms. "If you will excuse me, I have a letter to write."

He walked off and never looked back. Larry knew something had to be done but he wasn't sure how to accomplish it. He still had the feeling he had seen her before now, but where?

B.O. had just watched the exchange between Larry and Jam. He ran and caught up with Larry.

"Larry, where're you headed?" B.O. asked.

Larry turned his head and smiled. "To see you, my friend. We have some plans to make and information to gather."

"We do?"

"Yes, we do," Larry told him.

*J*am watched Larry and B.O. walk off together. She cursed in French. Then she looked down the road. She could not imagine what Larry saw in Susan. She had learned years ago how to pleasure a man. Jam had to have Larry, one way or another; she would use her body and make him beg for more.

Pat had also observed the exchange between Larry and Jam. She walked over to check on her.

"What's wrong with you?" Pat asked.

"Have you developed those pictures from the train station?" Jam returned the question.

"The ones of the nurses?" Pat answered with another question.

"Yes, I am interested in the group from England," Jam told her.

"Jam, you need to keep your mind clear and for the purpose we have been sent," Pat finally told her. "You're going to get us both killed. Stop this obsession with the American."

"Do not worry, my friend; our purpose is still the priority here," Jam said.

"Good, then stop thinking about Larry White and start thinking about the American plans," Pat said.

*S*usan faced the back of the truck until she could no longer see the man standing in the middle of the road. She could not believe all that happened last night. Susan remembered the story of how Sarah felt when Samuel went back to New York. She could now sympathize with her aunt's feelings. She was looking forward to the night out in New York after the war. She then turned and faced her friends, who were all smiling.

"Well, what did you guys think of the conference?" Nancy asked.

Susan, Pam, and Dawn all burst out into laughter.

"What's so funny?" Nancy asked.

"I am more interested in the physical aspects of Susan and Larry over the surgical techniques in the field," Pam said.

"He seems to be terribly interested in you, Susan," Dawn said.

"You two, maybe Susan wants to keep that information to herself," Nancy chastised her companions.

"Its fine, Nancy. Our families have quite a history," Susan told them.

"Really?" Nancy asked.

"How long a history?" Pam inquired.

"Our families have known one another for more than a hundred years," Susan answered.

Her three friends stopped their questions and stared.

"Did you say more than a hundred years? That explanation will take several nights," Pam said.

"I didn't make the connection that night at the USO," Susan said.

"The two of you looked like lovers the way you held onto one another all night," Pam said.

Susan's face turned red. She told her friends about the dinner in the truck, the trust money for her family, and the story of how his uncle and her aunt fell in love. The conversation made the return trip back to England go by quickly. They were met at the station by the same young private and taken back to camp. The "Georgia Peaches" quickly unpacked and prepared for the morning. They would be expected to give a full report. Dawn and Pam headed for the shower.

"I'm waiting until morning to shower. All I want is my bed," Susan told Nancy.

"Me too. I'm glad to be back here and away from that reporter," Nancy told Susan.

"Jam? I kind of liked her," Susan said.

"I don't trust her."

CHAPTER TWENTY-FIVE

*T*he "Georgia Peaches" had been called to Lieutenant Freedman's office. Susan opened a letter from Aunt Ida while they waited and found a picture of Angie and Jerry Leroy Long, Jr., born July fourth at one in the morning. He weighed six pounds, six ounces. Angie wasn't due until the fifteenth so his size was appropriate. Aunt Ida said all went well and there were no complications. Angie had sent a telegram through the Red Cross for Jerry. They did not expect the army to give him leave but Angie hoped for a call. Susan put the letter in her pocket when the door opened. Lieutenant Freedman entered the room; the women stood and saluted.

"Sit down, ladies. I have some important information for all of you," she told them.

They returned to their seats.

"Several months ago, when you were sent to the conference in Ireland, it was for a purpose. The four of you will be shipped out with a unit that will be arriving in two weeks. You need to prepare yourselves and return to my office next Monday for orders. At this time, that will be all the information I can give you, dismissed," Lieutenant Freedman told them.

The four women stood and left the office.

"Prepare ourselves, what does that mean?" Nancy said.

"It means we need to get our shit together and ready to go," Dawn told her.

"Susan, do you know anything? Any chance Larry might have slipped information to you?" Pam asked.

"No, and even if he did know, his letters, like mine, are censored. You know that," Susan answered.

"Well the good thing is we are all going together. I would hate to break up such a wonderful group," Pam said.

"The conference in Ireland makes sense now. We are about to be a part of something big," Nancy said.

"Good, I am ready for some action," Dawn told them.

Susan took the picture out of her pocket and looked at Angie and her nephew. The thought of never seeing him ran through her mind for a moment. The nightmares woke Susan with regularity now and she had begun to disturb Nancy. She blamed them on bad food or an upset stomach, but Nancy was not convinced.

"We need to start thinking of the items that may not be available—feminine pads, soap, toothpaste, and . . . " Susan told them.

"And another trip to The Culpeper house," Nancy said.

"We need to get busy," Susan said.

0800
Ireland

All the correspondents had been called to a meeting this morning. They had been waiting for weeks, some of them months, and now it seemed their assignments were about to be made. Larry was waiting for B.O. and hopefully information from home.

B.O. entered the building and found Larry. "I got it."

"Is it what I thought?" Larry asked.

"It's worse."

The major walked up to the podium. "Gentlemen and ladies, goodmorning, I have information for all of you at this time. In one week you will be given assignments and shipped out with your respected units. These assignments will not be traded or changed for any reason. You will all return here in one week at 0700 for your packets. I cannot answer any questions. Thank you," the major told the crowd of reporters and left the tent.

Jam looked at her friend and smiled. "Do you have any idea if we will be going the same place as Larry?"

"No, we are not, so if you still want to have sex with him do it quick. We have contacts to meet as soon as we land. Troop information and movement must be passed on. Maybe you can sleep with one of our kind instead," Pat told her.

"He has been friendly since his American whore left," Jam said.

"You are such a bitch. I am glad we are leaving here away from him and his friend. B.O. has been snooping around our tent more than I like," Pat told her.

"Maybe you should sleep with him, take away your stress," Jam suggested and smiled at her friend.

"Use your mind for a change instead of your body, would you?"

"Where is the fun in that?" Jam answered. She then looked up to see Larry and B.O. as they left the tent.

$\mathcal{L}$arry and B.O. walked to the mess tent and sat down.

"Larry, those bitches are spies," B.O. told him.

"Do we have enough proof to go to the general?" Larry asked.

"I don't think so; what I have is their affiliations while in college and some unexplained trips to the motherland," B.O. said.

"That's not enough. Something has been bothering me since I met her. I know I've seen her before. I have to get copies of my files from Hawaii and we have to get a picture of her," Larry said.

"I don't think that will be a problem," B.O. said and left the tent.

A few minutes later a small group of correspondents were standing together for a group shot. The main focus of the camera was on Jam and Pat. B.O. had the film developed within a few hours and then took the pictures to Larry.

"I have someone to send this to for a final identification, and then we can take it to the appropriate officers," Larry said.

"Whatever we need to do, it needs to be fast. We only have a week," B.O. reminded Larry.

"Friends in the radio room can help us out," Larry said.

"I hope what we get will be enough. They've had access to a lot of sensitive information that could lead to many American deaths," B.O. told Larry.

"I should have done this sooner."

Ellington Field
Houston, Texas

David took a moment before his meeting started to look at the reports he had accumulated over the last few months from the various bases on Dealer: 30-04-42, Alamogordo, New Mexico, 0900.

This officer observed Miss Johns enter the main hangar and exit where the C-47 was stationed. She was found hanging from the wheel well when she was approached and asked for reason to be in a secured area. Her explanation for being there was that she had lost her dog.

15-05-42, El Paso, Texas, 1500.

Miss Johns was found assisting the mechanics overhauling one of the motors on an AT-11 Expediter.

When approached by officers and questioned for her presence in a secured area, her answer was, "They asked me to help. I felt it was my patriotic duty."

The reports went on for every base they had been on. David had met a woman whose idea about women pilots ferrying planes to bases had impressed him. He had contacted her with Dealer's information and passion for flight. He would miss Dealer if she was accepted, but her abilities as a pilot would be needed in the months ahead.

There was a knock on the door. David looked up. An MP was standing at the door.

"Where did you find her?" he asked.

CHAPTER TWENTY-SIX

August 31, 1942
Ireland

Larry ran through the camp looking for his friend. They had to tell someone what had been uncovered before they were shipped out. He found B.O. in the mess tent eating.

"I got it. We have to go now, now! Damn it, now!" Larry screamed, and everyone in the tent turned and looked at him.

Larry had received the information on Jam and Pat. They both ran to the commanding officers' tent out of breath, requesting—almost demanding—an audience due to matters of security.

The general heard the commotion and walked out.

"Sir, please, just a moment of your time. It concerns two women who were sent out weeks ago. I have obtained troubling information as to their political associations with the Reich," Larry told him.

The general looked at Larry and B.O. "Your father is Jefferson Shaw, correct?" he asked.

"Yes, sir," Larry answered.

"Good man, I'll give you ten minutes," the general told them.

Larry and B.O. followed the general back into his office and sat down.

"Sir, there were two women here posing as reporters," Larry began.

"What do you mean posing?" the general asked.

"They obviously had the appropriate papers but their interest seemed out of place to me," Larry told him.

"The photographer named Pat was more interested in map rooms and equipment, and I discovered both had questioned many of the men and other reporters about their assignments," B.O. said.

"Why didn't you come forward before now?" the general asked.

"We didn't have enough, just speculation. It could have been passed off as journalistic curiosity," B.O. answered.

"While I was in Hawaii I wrote a number of articles on Hitler and his fanatical followers. My connections back home and overseas sent photographs of him during his rallies at a beer garden called the Hofbrauhaus and at Konigsplatz in Munich. We sent photographs of the two women to my contacts," Larry explained.

"And what were the results?" The general was becoming concerned.

"These," Larry answered. He then took the photographs of Jam and Pat at rallies, armbands and salutes captured on film. He presented the information on their college and social affiliations.

The general looked up at both men in disbelief.

"There's more." B.O. then presented a birth certificate on Pat Hentone, born and raised in Germany. "She's fluent."

The general stood, his face bright red. "How the hell did those women get clearance to be here? This information has come at a bad time. They have to be found now. Did either one of them tell you which assignment they were given?" he asked.

"No," they both answered.

The general walked out and looked at his clerk. "Get me the major who was in charge of assignments for the reporters and tell him to bring me his fucking paperwork now!"

CHAPTER TWENTY-SEVEN

1700, September 1, 1942
Amarillo, Texas
Amarillo Air Force Base

ealer stood outside her plane and watched Mr. Fines go inside. She had never seen a place so flat in her life, you could see from one county to the next. It was hot as hell here, too. Dealer took her hand and shaded her eyes to look around the base when she located the B-17. She stood there breathless. It begged to be explored, touched and savored by someone who could appreciate its ability under enemy fire. Dealer looked for MP's; seeing none, she began her stroll to the huge Flying Fortress.

What Dealer didn't see was the pair of eyes that watched as she disappeared into the wheel well.

"What the hell!" the captain said. He then went to find an MP to go with him to check on this intruder.

avid had just left the MP office and was headed for his meeting. He thought about the letter for Dealer in his jacket pocket. He wasn't sure when he was going to give it to her, but the opportunity would present itself.

As David entered Colonel Wayne Andrews' office he could see out the windows. He could see movement and saw a pilot and an MP headed to the B-17. He shook his head.

Colonel Andrews turned and looked out the window. "Problem, David?"

"Not for you, but my usual," David said and reached to shake an old friend's hand. "You look good, Wayne."

Wayne stood and walked to the window with David. "I am assuming this involves the notice we have all received about your wandering young pilot."

"She's harmless and very soon will be flying most of the planes she has checked out, so to speak," David said.

"The experimental women's ferrying program?" Wayne asked.

"Yes, I have her acceptance letter in my pocket."

"You must have a lot of faith in her, David."

"She's a damn good pilot and I hate to lose her, but Dealer will be an asset in that program," David answered.

"Should we watch this?" Wayne asked.

"No, we'll hear about it soon enough," David answered, and turned away from the window.

They sat down and began their meeting.

"Are there quarters available for the two of us? I have another meeting in Oklahoma before we return to Leland," David asked.

Wayne made a call. "Arrangements have been made, including dinner."

David tried to keep his mind on business but was very curious about what was taking place in the B-17.

ealer had dropped back out of the wheel well and found a side hatch that was open. It took three tries but she made it through and discovered this led to the cockpit. Dealer could not stop herself so she sat down in the pilot's seat and latched the belt. She thought she had heard noise in the back of the plane but fascination and curiosity kept her from investigating. She looked at all the dials and switches and started to reach for the throttle.

"I think you need a few phonebooks," the male told her.

She looked up to see two men, one an MP. She had to think quickly.

"I was told by the pilot to meet him here for a tour of the plane," Dealer said.

"Really?"

"Excuse me, but this . . . " the MP started to say something but the officer stopped him.

Dealer thought she might be able to pull this one off and got cocky. "Who are you to question the pilot of this plane?" Dealer asked.

*T*he officer looked at this spitfire sitting in his seat, impressed with her ability to lie so quickly when questioned. "Well, first, you are sitting in my seat, in my plane. I am the captain of this plane and I don't know you."

Dealer closed her eyes, dropped her head, and unlatched the belt. The captain looked at the MP and motioned for him to leave. "I can handle this; thank you for coming."

"Yes, captain," the MP saluted and left the plane.

"You have to be the pilot we have all heard about," the captain told her.

"My name is Dealer. I'm sorry," she said.

"Sorry you got caught, you mean? My name is Frank Bowen. Now that I know you're not a spy trying to steal my plane, would you like a real tour?"

"That would be great. I have so many questions! How do all these dials work? How . . ."

Frank answered Dealer's questions for almost an hour.

*D*avid and Wayne decided to walk out to the B-17 after their meeting. They were met in the hallway with a handwritten report from the MP. The report he was given said that the suspect was left with Captain Frank Bowen for further questioning.

David handed the report to Wayne, who began to laugh.

"What's so funny?" David asked.

"Captain Bowen has a reputation with the women," he answered.

"If this was anyone besides Dealer, I might worry."

Both men could see Captain Bowen leaning against a tire, looking into the wheel well on the left side of the B-17. Captain Bowen came to attention and saluted as both men walked up. Wayne burst into laughter as he watched Dealer lean out upside down with a wrench in her hand and grease on her face and salute him.

"Do you see what I mean?" David said. "Dealer, could you finish your work on Captain Bowen's plane and come down, please?"

"Right away," Dealer answered.

"Dealer, we will be staying overnight and have been invited for dinner at the officers' club," David told her.

"Captain Bowen, will you escort our guests to their quarters and bring them to the officers' club for dinner?" Colonel Andrews asked.

"Yes, sir," Frank answered and saluted.

Dealer climbed down, took the rag David handed her, and attempted to wipe the grease off her face. They obtained their bags and walked to a Jeep waiting in front of the main building. Dealer was dropped off at the women's quarters. A female took Dealer inside and assured Captain Bowen she would be brought to the officers' club.

ealer hadn't brought any dress clothes for dinner. She hoped what she had would be acceptable but doubted it. Dealer dropped her bag on the bed and looked into the mirror at the grease on her face. She went and turned on the shower; she only had an hour to get ready. Dealer ran back to the hallway.

"Excuse me; does anyone have something appropriate for me to wear to dinner?" Dealer asked the woman.

"I think we can fix you up," she answered.

aptain Bowen drove David to his quarters. As David got out of the Jeep he turned and looked at the captain.

"A suggestion, young man. Dealer is an experienced pilot who is very special to me. I expect you to be a gentleman. Do I make myself clear?" David told him.

"Yes, general, I understand."

"Your reputation precedes you," David turned and went inside the BLQ to dress for dinner.

2000
Officers' Club

*D*ealer could see Colonel Andrews, Mr. Fines, and Captain Bowen at a table having a drink when she walked into the club. She felt nervous about what she had borrowed from the ladies in the building. The black skirt fit nicely but the red top seemed snug and she had never worn heels like these. Dealer felt silly but the ladies who helped with the clothes said she was a peach. They combed Dealer's hair and pulled it back away from her face. Dealer took a deep breath and walked up to the table. All three men stood to greet her. She turned around to see who was behind her, and then heard the muffled laughter from the table.

"Dealer, you look different," David told her.

Captain Bowen pulled out a chair for her.

"I do?" she asked.

"In a nice way," Wayne said. "I apologize for not introducing myself at the plane earlier. I am Colonel Wayne Andrews."

"It's nice to meet you, Colonel."

Frank was stunned at the woman who stood before him. "You're lovely," Frank told her, offering a chair.

Dealer blushed and watched a man in a white jacket walk up to the table. "May I get you something to drink?" the waiter asked.

"A beer, please."

"What kind? We have a large variety," the waiter pointed out.

Dealer was embarrassed. Beer was beer, at least in Leland.

"Bring what you have on tap," Frank told the waiter.

"Thank you," Dealer told him.

David reached into his pocket and handed Dealer an envelope. "I was going to wait but I have something to give you. After today I feel now is the most appropriate time."

"You're going to fire me, aren't you?" Dealer asked and could feel tears in her eyes.

"It's more of a promotion," David said, and then looked at the other men at the table.

Dealer tried not to cry, took the letter, and opened it. She held her breath and looked at Mr. Fines. "This is real?" she asked.

"It's real and you will need to report for testing and a physical. If you pass, I believe the first class will be in November," David told her.

Frank watched the tears slip down her face. "May I?"

Dealer handed him the letter and looked back at Mr. Fines. "I have to find you another pilot."

"It won't be necessary. I am hoping Lewis will be able to take your place. I understand he taught you to fly," David said.

A bottle of champagne was brought to the table and opened. Dealer jumped when the cork popped. Glasses were poured and David stood.

"To Dealer. The air force will never be the same again. Congratulations."

"To Dealer," Wayne and Frank stood.

Dealer stood, wiped her eyes, and touched glasses, then drank.

They were shown to a table where dinner was ordered and the celebration continued.

As the main dish was served Dealer started to laugh; the men stopped and looked at her.

"What's so funny?" Frank asked.

"The pork," she said.

"Is there something wrong with your meal?" Wayne motioned for a waiter.

"Oh, no, I was thinking of a conversation my paw and I had about women pilots. He said when the military let women into planes, pigs would fly. I have to tell him they just grew wings."

Everyone at the table laughed.

*F*rank continued to observe the woman who sat next to him the rest of the evening. She was not the same person he had found a few hours ago seated in his plane. She was bright, intelligent, and a little rough around the edges, but that made her more interesting.

After dinner David and the colonel stood to leave. Frank stood.

"Captain, could you make sure Dealer is returned safely to her quarters?" David asked.

"Yes, General, I will be happy to do that."

"Dealer, I moved our meeting to noon. I will see you at 0900."

"I will be ready," Dealer said.

After David and the colonel left, Frank sat down.

"General, Mr. Fines is a general?" Dealer asked.

"Retired, but yes, a general," Frank told her.

"Wow, I didn't know."

"May I ask you a question?" Frank asked.

"I guess."

"What is your real name?" Frank asked.

"Deelyn."

"Deelyn, would you take a ride into town with me? I promise to be a gentleman and have you back safe and sound to your quarters," Frank asked.

Dealer smiled. "Okay, but we can't be gone long; I have a flight in the morning. Please call me Dealer. My parents are the only ones who call me Deelyn."

"Just an hour or two, I promise. You can tell me the reason you're called Dealer," he said.

The two left the club and Frank helped her into the Jeep. It was still warm outside and a slight breeze blew.

Dealer looked up into the sky and could see the outline of thunderheads. "Those might cause some issues if they aren't gone by morning," Dealer said and pointed to the clouds.

"I wouldn't mind another day to show you around," Frank said.

Frank and Dealer left the front gate and headed down Route 66.

"Amarillo is bigger than I thought, but is the whole city flat?" Dealer asked.

"Pretty much," Frank said and pulled into an A&W Root Beer drive-in.

The car next to them had the radio on. "You Stepped Out of a Dream," by Glenn Miller was being played.

Frank waved at a carhop who roller-skated to the Jeep. "We'll have two mugs, please."

Frank listened to Dealer describe home, family, her nickname and a passion for flying that surpassed his while they waited for their order.

"Where are you stationed?" Dealer asked.

"San Antonio for the moment, but not for long. Have you ever been there?"

"Which one? Kelly or Randolph?" Dealer asked.

"Randolph."

"I have been to both but never into the city," Dealer said.

"A shame. San Antonio is a beautiful city. You must allow me to show it to you one day," Frank told her.

"Maybe I will get stationed there if I pass," Dealer said.

"When you pass, you mean," Frank told her.

"You have never seen me fly."

"If you're good enough for the general you're good enough for the air force," Frank said. He looked at his watch and realized time had slipped away. "I better keep my promise and take you back." He waved for the carhop to pick up their mugs along with a tip.

The drive back to the base was filled with more questions about the B-17. Frank parked the Jeep in front of the women's quarters.

"I had a great time," Dealer told him.

Frank walked Dealer to the front door. Dealer stuck her hand out to shake his goodnight.

Frank took her hand, and leaned down and kissed her cheek. "Congratulations, I will see you before you leave in the morning."

Frank looked at her for a moment, then turned and walked back to the Jeep.

Dealer stood and looked at the man who had just kissed her. "I guess I should wear women's clothes more often," she said out loud.

0730, September 2

ealer returned the clothing and thanked the ladies. She was dressed in her travel clothes with one difference: she had pulled her hair back this morning. She walked out to find Frank waiting to take her to breakfast. She couldn't stop the smile that ran across her face.

"Do you have time for a fast breakfast?" Frank asked.

Dealer looked at her watch. "I think I can take time to eat," she said, then looked at the sky. It was clear; not a cloud in sight. But it was already hot. She threw her bag in the back of the Jeep, then hopped in. "Let's go, Captain."

"Yes, ma'am," Frank saluted.

Frank and Dealer had a quick breakfast, and then he drove her to the hangar. Her plane had been refueled and brought out. Dealer took her bag, threw it in the plane, and started her preflight check. When she finished, Dealer walked back, sat with Frank, and waited for Mr. Fines.

"When are you leaving?" Dealer asked.

"Today; I fly back to San Antonio, and after that it's classified," Frank told her.

"Think we will meet again?"

"If you keep in touch, probably," Frank told her.

"Give me your address," Dealer told him.

"I already did, last night on your acceptance letter."

"Pretty sure of yourself, aren't you?" Dealer said.

"Fly-boy," Frank answered.

"Are we ready to leave?" David asked.

Frank jumped up to attention. "At ease, Captain. I'm retired, remember?"

"Yes, sir. Permission to kiss your pilot?" Frank asked.

David was headed to the plane, and then turned at the question presented. "It's not my permission you need, son."

Frank turned around; Dealer reached out, grabbed Frank, and kissed him. "There. That's how we do it in Leland," she told him, then ran off.

"Good show, Dealer," David said.

"Thank you, General."

"When are you going to tell your family about the letter?" David asked.

"When we get back home. I have a favor to ask."

"You want me to be with you when you tell your father," David said.

"Yes, would you mind?" Dealer asked.

"It's the least I can do for you, Dealer. Sometimes it comes better man to man," David suggested.

Dealer took off and obtained clearance for an extra fly-by. She banked and flew over Frank one more time, then headed east on schedule. David smiled as he looked out the window.

*T*he flight crew for the B-17 walked up to where their captain stood.

Frank was lost in thought about the spitfire pilot from Mississippi who had a love for flying greater than his.

"What are you looking at, Frank?" his co-pilot asked.

"Do you men see that small plane east-bound?" Frank told them.

They all looked east at the plane quickly disappearing.

"Yes, sir," they all responded.

"My future wife is the pilot." Frank turned and headed toward the B-17 to start his preflight check.

"Frank Bowen married. The world is ending," his co-pilot said.

The rest of the men laughed and followed their captain to the plane.

"Captain," one of his crew called.

Frank turned around and stopped.

"Have you decided on the artwork for the nose of the plane? I am ready to start."

Frank looked eastward, and then smiled. "Yes, I will sketch it out once we are back at Randolph. I want it done before we leave the states."

CHAPTER TWENTY-EIGHT

November 6, 1942

The "Georgia Peaches," other medical personnel, and combat troops now traveled together on ship. They would be involved in Operation Torch. Susan and her friends had undergone weeks of intense training with their new unit. She felt they were as prepared as they could possibly be at this point in time. She had just read a letter from her sister in Houston about German U-boats seen in the Gulf of Mexico close to Galveston. Both of her brother-in-laws were on ships somewhere in the Pacific, or they could be on the same one she now stood. She would never know unless they ran into each other or until the war was over and they were allowed to discuss the past. Larry's last letter had him still stationed in Ireland, but that had been more than a month ago. Susan looked up as the door opened.

"Susan, have you seen Dawn or Nancy?" Pam asked.

"Nancy was making sure her uniform fit and Dawn was on her way to the head," Susan told her.

Nancy heard her name as she entered their small compartment "Pam, this fits like a glove. Thanks."

"Didn't Dawn take that stuff you made for us to help with the sea sickness? You are most welcome, Nancy. I guess all those sewing lessons paid off," Pam told her.

"No, but I bet she will now," Susan said. "Even B.O. took it."

"Glad to know he's going to be with us," Nancy said.

Dawn entered the room with a wet towel in her hand for her pale face. She stopped and dry-heaved into the trash.

"Are you ready to take what Susan made us?" Pam asked.

"How am I ever going to be able to swallow it?" Dawn returned the question.

"I need to stop the nausea first and then we will work on the sea sickness," Susan told her.

Susan went to her belongings and found what she hoped would help Dawn. She missed Aunt Sarah's journal but felt it would be safe somewhere besides the middle of the ocean. She thought about the last entry she had read just before she mailed it to New York.

June 1863

Middleburg, Virginia

Leona, Maud, and I have traveled back to an abandoned house to look for supplies. We have all become adept at stealing from strangers and the dead. I ask God for forgiveness each time. I found a garden and something I didn't expect. Uncle Mike's slave, Chloe, and several runaway slaves hiding, waiting for their guide. It was good to see her and baby Sarah. They are well and their location is safe with me. Left my lantern to help them on their journey.

SJB

She would get the journal after the war and see what his surprise was for her on their night out in New York, just the two of them. *Maybe this man will understand, someone I can bear my soul to and these nightmares will end.* She hoped they could discover more about their family history, how they were connected, and maybe Larry could write a story or a book on their ancestors. She smiled thinking about making love to him.

"Susan, hurry," Nancy called out.

Susan walked back to find Dawn's head in the trash, heaving. Susan took lavender and peppermint back to where she sat. Over the next few hours Susan used these oils to help relieve the nausea. Once the nausea began to subside Dawn was given a tea of chamomile that helped her sleep. Susan would use ginger and calamus to help over the next few days for the motion sickness. She hoped the book she brought about herbs of Europe would be beneficial in the days ahead. Somewhere in the bowels of the ship she thought she heard music—"Bless 'Em All," by Jimmie Hughes.

*L*arry read the telegram from B.O., who was now on a ship headed with other troops involved with Operation Torch. Jam and Pat had disappeared once they arrived with troops at their assigned location. Their pictures, information, and orders to arrest them if found had been sent out shortly after their meeting with the general.

"Sir, we are about to land. The plane you are looking for is preparing to leave," the young pilot told Larry.

Larry looked at his orders. They were landing in Ethiopia. The B-17 on the runway had seen enough recent action that it had been sent here for repair. He would have to hurry to catch up with the pilot and his crew.

*O*n the ground, Frank and his crew prepared to leave. Frank had finished his final check on the plane and inspected the repairs. Project 19 would be a valuable tool during the war.

"Captain, the reporter is about to land," his co-pilot Don said.

Frank looked up at the nose. The red-headed woman dealing cards with "Dealer" written beneath it had survived their last run.

"Jack did a good job," Frank said.

"Too bad he is being replaced with a reporter," Don replied.

"No one can replace Jack. I don't understand why a reporter and not a new gunner? I hope he isn't claustrophobic," Frank said, and watched the plane land with what could be a possible problem.

Frank didn't wait to meet his passenger. He opened the side hatch and slid through it. He sent Don to usher this man quickly to the plane. Frank had to get airborne and head toward the battle with the rest of the squadron; too much time had been lost already. Frank heard the back door shut and footsteps headed toward him. Don had just sat down when Frank turned to look at the civilian.

"You need to buckle up. I am Captain Frank Bowen, the rest you will learn as we head out."

Frank turned his focus back to the instruments and the details of his flight. Motors were started and the plane taxied down the runway.

"Welcome aboard, sir. My name is Robert and this is my baby," he shook the stranger's hand, and then patted the 50-caliber gun out the right side of the plane.

"It's good to meet you. I'm Larry."

"I'll introduce you to the rest later," Robert told him.

"Did the captain say his name was Bowen?" Larry asked.

"Yes, sir, Captain Frank Bowen from Waynesboro, Georgia," Robert told him.

"This can't be possible," Larry said.

November 10, 1942
Leland, Mississippi

*D*ealer had her suitcase ready to be loaded beneath the bus. Her entire family had come to town to tell her goodbye. She hugged her brothers and little sisters, then her uncle Lewis.

"Girl, you make us proud now, ya hear?" Lewis said.

"I will."

Jinny looked at her daughter and the tears began to flow. "I want you to write as much as possible after your studies. I have to know you are well. Deelyn, you can come home anytime you want."

"I know, Maw. I will write, I promise," Dealer said, then hugged and kissed her.

Butch walked over and handed his daughter twenty dollars. "It ain't much but we took a collection among the family, and Mr. Fines pitched in too. Lewis is going to fly him while you're gone," Butch told her, then took out a red work rag and blew his nose.

Dealer looked at the money. "Paw, this is a lot of money. I feel bad about taking it when there are so many without."

"No, Deelyn, you might need that for something. You keep it and save it for a rainy day," Butch told his daughter.

"Time to go, folks," the bus driver said to those still standing outside the bus.

Dealer hugged her paw tight and kissed him on the cheek. She didn't say anything out of fear that the tears she held back would flow. She walked up the steps and found a seat by the window. Dealer waved at her family.

Butch walked over to his wife and put his arm around her. "Jinny, she will be all right. If anyone can fly those planes it's Deelyn."

The Johns waited until they could no longer see the lights of the bus, and then turned for home.

Dealer took an oil rag and wiped away the tears, leaving a smudge on her cheek. She looked at the letter with all the instructions on it for the training at Ellington. There would be someone to meet her at the station, and then take her to quarters that were arranged for the pilots. Her sadness was exchanged for thoughts of flight and a letter she had yet to read from Frank. Dealer smiled when she looked at the picture of the nose art on the B-17. Frank and his crew stood beneath the plane, smiling. She had so many thoughts about her future and the man who had called her lovely one September night in Amarillo, Texas.

White Daily Journal
New York

Emmitt sat in the office and looked over stories about to go to print. The *Journal* was being run almost entirely by women. They were doing an excellent job and the newspaper ran smoothly without men, much to his surprise. One of the female reporters had obtained information giving the *Journal* an exclusive, beating all other newspapers in New York. Emmitt's poor eyesight and childhood leg injury kept him out of the military. He felt proud to do what he could in the community and with the paper to help the war effort.

Emmitt began to look through the mail that arrived that morning. He almost opened a package addressed to Larry, but then looked at the return address and saw Susan Bowen's name. He thought about the history between the Bowen family and his and wondered if there was more than they had been told as children. He was upset with Larry for not staying in Hawaii. Their mother worried every day over Larry and his need to report on the war. It had been weeks since the family had received a letter from him, most of which was censored. *Why write if you know it's going to be blacked out?* he thought. Emmitt was curious about the package but turned, opened the old safe that once belonged to Grandfather, and placed it with the rest of the White history. It would be safe until Larry returned from the war.

"Boss, one of the printers is acting up again," an older man said.

"Get Nona. She fixed it the last time," Emmitt told him.

November 16, 1942
Ellington Field
Texas

ealer stood with the other women and repeated her oath, in the size forty-four zoot suit that had been issued to everyone. She had rolled the pant legs and sleeves up as far as possible and hoped the belt would hold until she could find someone to help alter it. Dealer never learned any sewing or mending skills growing up, but now she wished she had listened to her maw.

"Don't worry, Dealer. When we get back to the tourist courts tonight I can fix these things we're wearing," Thelma told her.

Thelma Stanley was Dealer's assigned roommate. Thelma was the opposite of Dealer—tall, black hair, dark eyes, and carried a California tan. The two hit it off the moment they met. "For the love of flying," they toasted one another with their first beer at a local bar not far from where they lived.

"We have to do something. I can't walk around like this the entire time we're in school," Dealer responded.

"All I need is some thread and a pair of scissors. It will look good when I am done," Thelma reassured her.

"Looking at all these uniforms you might be busy making us all look good," Dealer said.

"I could use a little extra spending money."

The two laughed, then walked into the classroom where introductions took place, the importance of the program was discussed, and then school really began. By the end of the day Dealer was glad she had sent letters home and to Frank. It might be a while before they got another one from her.

CHAPTER TWENTY-NINE

2300, December 31, 1942
Front Line, North Africa
Evacuation Unit

*S*usan sat on her cot and watched her roommates sleep as the rain beat down in a steady rhythm. She had managed to keep them all healthy with echinacea and extra garlic. Susan had made tea of valerian and lavender to help with the fatigue they all suffered. Some of the other nurses had not been so fortunate and became ill from harsh weather conditions and exhaustion. A few had been admitted to the hospital and two had been sent back home, which now left them short-staffed.

There would be no celebration of a new year tonight, just a little extra sleep for the weary. She thought about how war had changed the face of the holidays for those at home and far away. Susan had written so many letters for her patients and knew her aunt had done the same during the Civil War.

She thought of her family in Waynesboro and had honored her Aunt Ida's request. She said a prayer every night, even if it was while she stood in surgery. Susan prayed for all the nurses at the front who worked endless hours in the worst of conditions with dwindling supplies. She thought about the doctors who had not yet realized the full potential of these women and their bravery under enemy fire. Each time Susan thought she had seen the worst man could do to man, another ambulance would arrive with new horrors and new challenges.

Angie's letters detailed the changes that were taking place in the states. Women had left their homes to work in the factories and stepped out into a man's world and into history. Those who chose to make a difference would possibly change the way the nation looked at women and what they were capable of accomplishing now and in the future. Aunt Sarah had said the same thing about the women who had traveled away from home to go to heal.

"Susan, what are you doing? It's late," Nancy asked.

"Just thinking."

Nancy sat up on her cot. "Thinking about your family?"

"My sisters, brother, Larry . . . "

"Bill?" Nancy asked.

Susan didn't answer, but she was worried about Bill. "Nancy, I worry about everyone who is involved in this war, including us. What happened between Bill and me is over. I'm looking forward to my date in New York when the war ends," Susan smiled.

"If you two are going to talk all night I guess we might as well bring in the New Year together," Dawn said. "Pam, wake up."

"I have been awake since Susan came into the tent," Pam responded.

"What time is it?" Nancy asked.

"Midnight," Susan answered.

"Happy New Year," the four said one to another. A few banters of resolutions and promises to stay together throughout the war were made by everyone, and then one by one lanterns were turned out.

Susan's lantern was the last to be extinguished. She covered herself with a blanket and listened to the steady breathing of her friends. As she drifted off to sleep, somewhere she heard music of Billie Holiday singing "God Bless the Child."

*I*n a farmhouse on occupied German land another celebration was taking place between friends. Jam passed a bottle of red wine to her friend along with the loaf of bread she had found as they rummaged through the house.

"Happy New Year, my friend," Jam said.

"Same to you," Pat responded.

Both women laughed as they gathered food and blankets, and then left the house. Jam turned, lit the rag on a bottle filled with gasoline, and threw it in the house. It would burn any evidence of them being there and the two dead partisans inside. They would now claim their identities and continue to disappear deeper into the inner workings of the French resistance.

CHAPTER THIRTY

0600, Sunday, February 14, 1943
Thala, North Africa

First Lieutenant Lisa Fields had just obtained information about the battle at Faid Pass from her superior. She needed to get her people together, and fast. She looked up and saw Nancy walking across the compound.

"Nancy, go find your friends and tell anyone else you run into that we are about to be busy," Lisa said.

"Yes, ma'am," Nancy responded, and ran to her tent. "We have to go now," Nancy said, then looked for the others.

"Where?"

Dawn was using the marigold cream Susan had made for her on a rash at the back of her neck when Nancy ran into the tent. "Susan went to get mail and Pam is in the mess tent."

"How's the rash?"

"Just about gone. You know I never dealt much with herbs or natural healing until now," Dawn said.

"Neither have I since my father is a physician, but Susan has changed the way I will look at nature and its healing properties." Nancy pulled her hair back out of her face, preparing for work.

"What's going on?" Pam asked as she entered their tent and gave Dawn a cup of coffee.

"German offensive, we have to go," Nancy told her.

"Shit!" Pam said.

"What's wrong? No, you didn't!" Dawn asked.

"Well I won't be getting that day off," Pam said.

"You didn't get all the instruments done, did you?" Nancy asked.

"No."

"No what?" Susan asked, coming into the tent with a handful of mail, dandelions, and rose hips.

"Oh, nothing much, we have wounded coming and Pam here didn't get the instruments done," Dawn answered.

"Lieutenant Fields is going to kill me," Pam said.

"Or make you inventory the supply room again," Nancy responded.

"Stop worrying. I finished them late last night before my shift was over in the ward," Susan told them.

"I owe you," Pam told her.

Susan smiled. "I will take you up on that the next time Larry is around or you have an extra pair of nylons."

"What are you doing with the weeds and those red things?" Dawn asked.

"Those weeds and berries are going to help keep all of us from getting scurvy or sick," Susan answered.

"Where did you get them? It's too early, isn't it?" Pam asked.

"Oh, I have made a few friends outside the camp," Susan answered

"Susan, you need to be careful. You can't trust everyone," Nancy said.

"I didn't go alone. B.O. went with me."

Nancy looked out of the tent. "Let's go. Ambulances are pulling up."

The "Georgia Peaches" left their tent and met up with other nurses to start what would be the beginning of a very long day and night.

Houston, Texas

*D*ealer sat on the edge of her bed in a black dress, looking at the photograph of her family. She and the other women knew there was always a possibility they could be injured or die. Accidents happened. The last few days at Ellington had been difficult on everyone.

"Dealer, we need to go," Thelma told her.

"Just a minute, I need to get something," Dealer said, and took the twenty-dollar bill she had saved all these months out of her Bible. "I thought the government would help us in times of need, but I guess we will have to help ourselves."

"Eileen was a good friend and a damn good pilot," Thelma responded, and took ten dollars out her button box.

"I hope we will be able to get enough money for the train fare. It wouldn't be right to not get her body home to her family," Dealer said.

There was a knock on their door. Both women picked up their Bibles and left with the rest of the women pilots for the church where Eileen's funeral service was about to take place. Dealer went back to turn the radio off but changed her mind when she heard "Amazing Grace."

Ethiopia

Frank Bowen sat with Larry, drinking coffee, watching his plane being repaired and prepped for another mission. The conversation he had just had with the reporter had taken him by surprise.

"My sister, are you sure?" Frank asked.

"Susan Bowen, nurse, home is in Waynesboro, had a great aunt who traveled battle-to-battle healing during the Civil War," Larry said.

"Yep, that's Susan. What is she doing? Trying to get killed?"

"I believe she is doing what is in her heart and in her blood from the stories she told me about her great aunt," Larry said.

"We have all heard the stories about Aunt Sarah and the reporter."

"Well that reporter was my ancestor; our families have known each other for more than a hundred years," Larry told him.

Frank shook his head in disbelief. He remembered thinking Larry might be a problem when he had been forced to take on this civilian. Frank still wasn't sure why Larry was flying with them, but orders were orders. "I want to thank you for helping out when we got hit. If it hadn't been for you my co-pilot would be dead."

Larry didn't answer but looked at the letter in Frank's hand. "Wife?"

Frank smiled. "One day."

"You seem pretty sure about that," Larry told him.

"Fate," Frank responded.

"I never believed in fate until I met your sister."

CHAPTER THIRTY-ONE

April 24, 1943
Houston, Texas
Ellington Field

D ealer sat in the warm sun of a Houston afternoon and waited with the other pilots to receive their wings. She knew her family was in the crowd. She worried about Frank, as they received information almost daily about planes going down, their crews dead or missing. His last letter had been written on Valentine's Day. As usual, not much information, just his early congratulations on her graduation and the rest censored.

"Deelyn Ernest Johns," her name was called from the stage.

"Dealer, go. Everyone is waiting," Thelma told her.

"Oh, I didn't hear them."

Dealer stood, straightened her uniform, and walked to the stage where silver wings were pinned on a blue uniform. She turned and looked out across the sea of people and found her parents. Dealer knew her maw was holding back tears and she saw her paw take out a red work rag and blow his nose. What surprised her was to see General Fines sitting with them.

"D eelyn," Butch called out. "Now, Jinny, stop your crying; you don't want to upset Deelyn."

"I am so proud of her," Jinny said.

Everyone from the Johns family was present and watched as Dealer walked graciously over to them. Butch could see the tears in her eyes.

"It's so good to see all of you. I have missed everyone so much," Dealer told them.

Butch and Jinny held their daughter.

"Enough of this blubbering. Where are you going to be stationed at, girl?" Lewis asked.

"I am not sure yet. My roommate, Thelma, went to go pick up our paperwork. It will be a ferrying base, I do know that," Dealer said.

"Dealer, congratulations," David said as he walked up and handed her an envelope.

"Thank you, General."

"Dealer, I have our papers," Thelma told her.

"You first," Dealer told her.

Thelma tore open the packet. "I'm staying here! In Texas."

"Where?"

"Here at Ellington," Thelma answered.

"Well open up yours," Butch told her.

"Yes, maybe they will station you back in Mississippi," Jinny said.

The family watched Dealer tear open her packet.

"I can't believe this, Thelma, I have been stationed here, too," Dealer said smiling.

"Guess we better look for a place to live then," Thelma said.

Butch and Jinny could see the excitement in their daughter's face.

"Well at least you're close," Jinny said.

ealer spent the rest of the day with her family and the general. Thelma left with her family and both agreed to talk about an apartment the following day.

"Dealer, I need to go, but will see you and your family at breakfast tomorrow," David said.

"Paw, is everyone staying overnight?" Dealer asked.

Butch smiled at his daughter. "Mr. Fines put all of us up in a fancy hotel in town. He said it was the least he could do for taking our daughter."

Dealer looked at the general.

"There is a room for you, too. You deserve it. Bring your friend Thelma. There is a band playing tonight and I reserved a table for you and your family."

Dealer walked over and hugged the general. "Thank you."

"You're welcome."

Dealer found Thelma at the tourist courts when she returned for an overnight bag.

"What are you doing here?"

"My family had to leave," Thelma answered.

"Well I have a free room in a fancy hotel downtown and a re-served table in the bar," Dealer said smiling.

"Room for one more?" Thelma asked.

"What are friends for?" Dealer asked and laughed.

"Let me get some things," Thelma said.

Dealer sat down, took the envelope the general had given her, and opened it. Inside was a hundred dollars along with a letter.

Congratulations,

I never had a doubt or concern you would get your wings.

Your assignment was not by chance. Over the next six months work very hard and learn all that you can.

I will be in touch. There are plans in the future that involve you.

Be safe.

David Fines

Dealer said nothing, folded the letter, and placed it and the hundred dollars in her Bible.

CHAPTER THIRTY-TWO

October 1943
Southern England

*F*rank smiled as he looked at the pictures of Dealer in her uniform at graduation with her wings and the one of her in her flight suit.

"We're ready, Captain," Don told him. "Pictures from home?"

Frank put the pictures in his pocket. "Deelyn's graduation pictures; she is now officially a WASP. At least she is safe. Where's our passenger?"

"Right here," Larry said.

"Everyone is aboard, sir," Robert said.

"This is going to be another bad one, so everyone get ready," Frank said.

"Is there any other kind?" Don asked.

Paris
Gestapo Offices

*C*ommandant Hans Schmidt had not been convinced when one of the Maquis demanded in German to speak with him. The story about infiltrating the French resistance was something he had heard before. The French resistance had many individuals who spoke several languages, and fluently. Their papers looked authentic, the code word was correct, and he had made several phone calls to verify they were who they claimed. Now he would have to wait for responses. He had the two women under guard in the adjoining room.

Hans wanted them close, and if they were not who they claimed he would shoot them. He could hear their chattering from the next room.

"Why is this taking so long?" Jam asked. "We have been here since dawn."

"We were told this might happen if we were caught," Pat reminded her. "He can't just take our word; there are procedures he must follow."

"You are sure about the code word?" Jam asked.

"Yes, I'm sure. Why?" Pat asked.

The commandant received a reply to his last call. It had taken most of the day to collect his information. He stood, straightened his uniform, entered the room, and looked at both women.

"Your papers have been authenticated, my apologies," Hans said, and looked at the aide standing in the door. "Bring wine and food to my office immediately."

"Completely understandable, since this is the first time we have been detained," Jam responded.

"In the past there were no survivors and we simply moved on," Pat said.

Hans was impressed these women were able to kill and discuss it openly, an admirable trait in his opinion. "You both have influential friends at the highest level. The report I received indicated your work so far has been beneficial to the Reich."

"We have much work left to do," Pat said.

Jam walked over to a table where food and wine had been brought. She picked up the bottle of wine, "French, and a good year."

Pat joined her friend. "It has been a while since we enjoyed such delicacies," Pat said, and took the glass Jam offered her.

Jam turned to the commandant and smiled. "Join us; we have much to celebrate."

The officer looked at Jam and returned the smile. "Thank you, maybe later. Come see what your handy work has accomplished for your fuhrer, and with your continued efforts we can stop this trash."

Pat and Jam watched as ten Maquis were lined up and forced to kneel outside Gestapo headquarters.

"We cannot seem to arrest or catch more than two or three of these bastards at any one time," Hans said. "It takes too long to capture and execute them to be of any use. For everyone we shoot four more take his place."

"Yes, we have never seen more than three traveling together. It is part of their training; less information travels with fewer individuals," Jam said.

"For the fatherland," Pat said, and raised her glass.

"Heil Hitler," Jam said, and saluted as one by one each man was executed. "Pat, we cannot go back without appearing to have been questioned."

"Have you heard of Ravensbruck?" Hans asked.

"The female concentration camp?" Pat returned the question.

"Yes. I have some things from there that will assist you. We will change your clothing but to make it appear you have been questioned will require I am afraid some discomfort for both of you. I can have the medical staff sedate you before proceeding."

"No!" Pat said.

"We do this for our fuhrer," Jam said proudly.

"It would be my honor if you two would join me for dinner this evening. Tomorrow you may leave to continue your work for our fuhrer," Hans walked over and kissed Jam's hand.

"But we have no proper clothing, commandant," Jam said.

"My name is Hans, and I believe that can be arranged."

Pat looked at her reflection and knew tomorrow she would be dressed in rags, bruised, and probably sleeping on the ground. Tonight she would enjoy a roof over her head, good food, wine, and the company of her people. The only cost would be Jam sharing her body and sexual perversions with the commandant.

"Jam, you need to hurry," Pat told her friend.

"You never learn. Men expect women to be late; its part of our mystique, the game we play to get what we want or need."

"I am going to regret not being able to bathe and sleep in a bed, but the rewards will be great when this war is over and our fuhrer commands the world," Pat said.

She watched Jam put on a piece of jewelry that had belonged to someone else and spray perfume between her breasts.

"I am counting on those rewards. Shall we? I believe the men are waiting for us," Jam said.

"You should enjoy this evening. Tomorrow will not be so pleasant for either of us," Pat said.

"Large amounts of French wine, a little sexual role play, and any discomfort will become easier to endure."

Frank sat in a small cave remembering the last thing he saw as he slid out the side hatch of his B-17. The sight of the red-headed dealer in flames would be imprinted forever in his mind. He felt lucky to be alive. Frank hoped to find his way into land occupied by the allies and his men. It had been a day and night since his plane went down; he was cold and hungry. He reached in his pocket to make sure the pictures of Deelyn were still there and intact. The sun had set; maybe tonight he could find food and better accommodations. Frank made his way out into the night once again.

"Please do not move," the male voice said with a French accent.

"I am American," Frank told him.

"Is your name Bowen?"

"Yes."

The man lowered his gun, turned, and spoke French.

Frank watched as men and women appeared out of nowhere. "Please come, my name is Claud and we are the Maquis; you are safe with us."

Frank followed this group through the woods and to a small farmhouse. He watched as the others disappeared into the trees. Frank followed Claud inside the house where he heard familiar voices from the three men sitting at the table. The three stood and grabbed Frank's hand.

"Frank, it's good to see you," Larry said. "We heard there was someone wandering in the woods."

Frank looked to see not only Larry but Don and Robert. "Is there anyone else?"

"Captain, right now we are the only ones who have been found alive," Don said.

"I, for one, am happy to be here," Robert told him.

Frank listened to Larry speak French to Claud. "Well that's handy."

"And useful. We have to change clothes so that we look like everyone else. Our survival will depend on it," Larry told him.

"You're not just a reporter, are you?" Frank asked.

"Let's just say there are two problems that need to be found before more damage is done. You and your men were not intended to become a part of this."

"Maybe you should explain what my superiors have failed to do," Frank told him.

Frank listened over the next hour to what Larry had to say about two spies and his volunteering to be dropped behind enemy lines and contact the Maquis. "So your trips with us have been preparations?"

"Yes, I regret the loss of your plane and men."

"I hope your side trip will be worth the cost of my men." Franks voice was filled with anger.

"If I can't help stop these bitches, more Maquis will die. The information we get from them is invaluable for our troops in the field," Larry said. "I could use your help but it's your choice."

"Captain Bowen, my brother and nine other men were executed at Gestapo headquarters in Paris, their bodies burned. The two women who were with my brother are these spies. They were rewarded and spent the night entertaining the bastards who killed our friends," Claud told him.

"And your proof these are the same women? How do you know they entertained the Germans?" Frank asked.

Larry took the photograph of Jam and Pat and showed it to him.

"The women in this picture are the same two who have lived, fought, and pretended to be Maquis for months," Claud said. "The Germans are not the only ones who have spies. The tall one slept with the commandant and both were dressed and made to appear as if they had escaped from the authorities. They were driven by Gestapo and let out into the countryside to rejoin and continue their work as Maquis."

"Captain, Robert and I discussed this before you were found. We want to help," Don said. "But you are in charge. It's your decision and we will follow your orders."

Frank was angry he had been kept out of the decision-making process for his men, but as a soldier he followed orders. "Do I have a choice?"

"Yes, you do, and if you choose not to go with me I will make sure you and your men are taken safely to allied lines," Larry said.

Frank thought about Deelyn, his family, his men, and these people who had found him. "We'll stay and help."

"Welcome," Claud said. "Wine and bread for our new friends. Eat, and then we will begin our search."

CHAPTER THIRTY-THREE

November 23, 1943
Sicily

Susan stood with the "Georgia Peaches" and the rest of their unit, preparing to board an army transport. They were heading to England with the distinction of being the most experienced hospital in the US Army. She read a letter from her friend Judy and discovered that they had been within a few miles of each other. Judy had joined the army and was working in a segregated hospital. Susan shook her head. She could not understand the reasons to separate one race from another. When someone was injured it mattered not; what mattered was to save lives. She and Judy had treated all races in Chile—the color of their skin made no difference—it was to relieve the pain and suffering, to care for all who came seeking help.

Judy had dismissed her previous love for a new one. His name was Isaiah and he was a Tuskegee airman. Judy had a ring and would send a picture in her next letter. Susan had heard of the all-black air corps. When they got to England she would write and tell Judy how close they had been to one another. Judy sent her love and continued prayers for all involved in the war.

Susan folded the letter and thought about what they had been through since February. Tunisia, Algeria, then to Sicily. She remembered passing bodies during the summer that were bloated, rotting in the summer heat, waiting to be collected by the graves' registration crews. Susan thought about her aunt and wondered if she had seen the same. She must have—the battles, hundreds of bodies decaying in the hot sun. Aunt Sarah must have gone through the same scenes and retained those memories of death. The same memories she would never forget.

There were other battles they fought that did not include weapons. The weather had caused problems. Storms had left equipment ruined, and the standing water bred mosquitoes, which then brought malaria. The nurses were not immune and several in their company became sick. She had been prepared and gathered neem, yellow root, and herb Robert while in Africa. Susan treated her friends and any of the other nurses who asked. They had been lucky and the book she bought in England had been beneficial.

"Nancy, what did the lieutenant say we were being assigned to again?" Dawn asked.

"European Theater of Operations," Nancy answered.

"Something to do with the next invasion," Pam said.

"Any idea how long we will be in England?" Dawn asked.

"No one knows at this time but any chance to rest is welcomed," Susan told them.

"Agreed. Any word from Larry?" Nancy asked.

"No, and I am worried."

The women climbed aboard and found their spot for the trip to England. Susan looked up and saw B.O. coming toward them.

"You're like a bad penny, you just keep showing up," Susan said and laughed, but then noticed he wasn't smiling. "What's wrong?"

"I need to talk to you," B.O. told her.

The rest of the "Georgia Peaches" surrounded them.

B.O. looked at all of them. "I just got this report, I'm really not supposed to say anything but I . . . "

"Larry?"

"Sit down, all of you; I think there are a few things you need to know. When all of you came to Ireland for the conference . . . " B.O. continued his story about Jam and Pat, their associations, and that Larry asked to be sent behind enemy lines to find the Maquis. He was to warn them and find the spies.

"I knew it. I never did like that tall witch," Nancy said.

"But why Larry?" Susan asked.

"He felt responsible that we didn't stop them before they were shipped out. They have caused a lot of damage and many Maquis have died because of them. Larry is fluent in French and Italian and can identify both of them. The army ran him through a rapid survival-training course before he left. Should I go on?" B.O. answered.

"Why didn't you go with him?" Pam asked.

"No experience jumping out of planes. Larry, on the other hand, is quite the athlete and dare devil," B.O. said.

"Why are you telling me now?" Susan asked.

"Because the B-17 he was traveling in went down."

"Survivors?" Dawn asked.

"We don't know," B.O. said.

Nancy walked over and wrapped her arm around Susan's shoulders.

"Susan, don't even think about it. Do you hear me?" Pam said.

"That's not the only reason I am telling you this." B.O. looked at Susan. "The captain of the B-17, his name is Bowen, Captain Frank Bowen.

1700
Dealer and Thelma's apartment
Houston, Texas

"*D*ealer, where are you going? Did they tell you?" Thelma asked.

"No, just that I needed to take my flight gear and report back to the airfield at 2000," Dealer answered. She had been ordered not to discuss anything other than she was leaving. Dealer knew she might be gone for a while, maybe a month.

"My, this is quite the mystery," Thelma said.

"Yeah, just like 'The Shadow,'" Dealer smiled. "It must have something to do with the extra training I have been going through."

"Well good luck and I will see you when you get back."

"Here, take this; it will cover the rent through December. If you need more there is an envelope in my Bible. Take what you need," Dealer handed Thelma money.

"So this is not just an overnight trip?" Thelma asked.

"I don't think so."

1800
Ellington Field
Houston, Texas

avid Fines, dressed in clothing for the flight overseas, walked away from the C-47 and straight into the commander's office. He was told upon his arrival the major was having dinner with his wife at the officers' club. This did not sit well, as information had been sent about his arrival.

"Call him and tell him to return immediately! He was ordered to be waiting for my arrival," David said.

The aide looked at him and picked up the phone to call the club. "Who shall I say is waiting?"

"General Fines . . . and I don't like to wait."

David stood in the major's office and watched as the Jeep pulled up to the front door thirty minutes later. David was not impressed when he entered the office, failed to salute, and sat down. David walked over and dropped the envelope on his desk. He watched the major open it and began reading the orders signed by the president.

"A matter of the security for the country?" the commander asked.

"Yes," David said.

"And that is all you are going to tell me. You intend to just walk out of here and take my best pilot?"

"Yes, Major, that is exactly what I am going to do," David said and then leaned across the desk. "And major, I would suggest the next time you are ordered to be somewhere you are there."

"I don't take orders from retired military personnel," the major stood.

"As of this morning, by presidential order, I am no longer retired. I have been returned to active duty," David said.

The major stood, saluted, and attempted to apologize. "I didn't know we had no notice of your status."

"There was no reason to notify you. This matter is out of your hands and in mine. One more thing, major, if I were you I would not look for a promotion anytime soon," David said and left the office. He returned to the C-47 where Dealer was standing with her flight bag.

"General Fines, it's good to see you," Dealer said, and saluted out of respect.

"It's good to see you, too," David returned her salute.

"Do you know why I'm here?" Dealer asked.

"Do you remember the letter I gave you at graduation?"

"Yes."

"Well, it's time for you to know about those plans," David said.

The captain of the C-47 came to the door. "General, we're ready to go."

"General, you returned my salute. Why are you dressed in uniform?" Dealer asked.

"A favor I owe has been called due," David said. "Dealer, we need to go."

"Where are we going?" Dealer asked.

"First to England, then you're going to France."

ealer sat and stared at the floor. She needed to send a message to her folks to let them know she wouldn't be home for Christmas, and she had to get more money to Thelma for their rent. England, France, maybe she would run into Frank. It had been a while since she had received a letter.

"Dealer, Dealer! I need you to read this; it will explain the future and your part in it," David said.

"General, my parents, Christmas, my rent," Dealer's words were fragmented.

"Taken care of when I saw them this morning. They think you are going to a military base in Alaska to teach. Your rent has been taken care of until you return. Sorry, this is classified—need-to-know only," David told her.

Dealer took the packet, opened it, and began to read. She stopped and looked at General Fines.

"I know what you're thinking, and yes, I knew you could read, write, and speak French since you were six years old," David said.

"The background check, the pages of questions about our family and history," Dealer said.

"The background check was standard but what it revealed is why you are here now. The extra training for weapons and communications are part of this operation. I had to fight to get you; don't let me down. You'll be a part of history."

Dealer never thought much about speaking French. Maw had been born and raised on the bayous in Louisiana. French was spoken every Sunday after church. All the Johns children could speak French and all of them could shoot whatever was placed in their hands, from guns to bows. Dealer realized the importance of what she was reading and the part she would play.

"The Jedburghs, that's what I have been training for?" Dealer asked.

"Yes, the Jedburghs."

CHAPTER THIRTY-FOUR

December 10, 1943
England

"Jf you say anything about my mother again I will cut your balls off," Dealer said in French, as she got off the British soldier that insulted her mother in the same language. She took her boning knife and replaced it. A small trickle of blood could be seen just below his Adam's apple.

General Fines and his British counterpart stood watching the test they had arranged for her.

"Scrappy young lass, we leave Monday at 0030."

David smiled. "We'll be there."

"I wasn't informed you were jumping, General."

"I'm not; just going along for the ride. I have a vested interest," David replied.

"Good show."

Midnight
France

Jam and Pat had been wandering and searching for several nights, looking for Maquis contacts. They had hidden in barns and built shelters in the woods for protection from the elements.

"What the hell is going on, Jam?" Pat asked.

"I'm not sure, my friend, but I would feel better if we could find at least one group to contact," Jam answered.

The two were huddled in a small root cellar behind the small farmhouse, hiding from the old woman who lived there.

"Ever since we left Paris the pockets of fighters have not been where the last scout said they would be located. It's like we are marked. Who else knew we had infiltrated the Maquis? Did you tell anyone else in Paris that night? Maybe let it slip while you were guzzling your French wine?" Pat demanded.

"Screw yourself, I told no one," Jam was hurt but Pat was right—they had been most unfortunate since leaving Paris.

"We have to get inside the house," Pat said.

"I'm going to relieve myself. I'll catch up at the house. The woman inside is old; she will die quick," Jam said. Jam exited the root cellar and proceeded into the trees.

Pat left the cellar and walked around to the front of the house. She was trying to think of a story to tell the old woman to get inside. She would cut her throat quickly. Pat could see a candle burning on the table. The old lady was drinking wine and stumbled to the door when she knocked.

"Hello, I am lost and in need of food and shelter. Will you help one who wishes only for the return of our country to its people?" Pat asked.

The old woman said nothing but opened the door for Pat to enter. When Pat turned to attack the old woman she came face to face with Larry White and too many guns pointed at her to do anything but drop her knife.

"Hello, Pat. Where's your friend?" Larry asked.

*J*am headed back to the farm house when the sound of American voices stopped her movement. She remained hidden and hoped to obtain valuable information from them. "I will be happy when we catch these women," Don said.

"Me, too. I am ready to get back and start flying again," Robert said.

"How did Larry find out about them being here tonight?" Don asked.

"Not sure, but this was set up to catch them. One down one to go, then we can get some R&R," Robert said.

Jam sat and listened, Larry here, looking for them. It had to be him who had ruined their infiltration back into the Maquis and now he had her friend. She would follow them and help Pat escape. She was sure they would not harm her friend. The Maquis would want as much information as possible from Pat. At the moment the door opened, Pat was brought out, tied to a tree, and shot. Jam almost screamed.

"Damn, I guess she didn't have anything to say," Robert said.

"Who shot her?" Don asked.

"Claud, it was his brother who was executed in Paris, remember?" Robert asked.

"Shit, remind me not to get on his bad side," Don replied.

Jam watched as her friend's body was doused with oil and set on fire. She could see Larry standing next to her friend's murderer. Jam thought they had been careful in Ireland, but somehow Larry found out. She could not believe this was a man she wanted to give her body to at one time. She tried to think amidst the hurt and loss of her friend. *Bastard has taken my friend away from me. I will find what is important to him, that which he loves, and take it.* She would have to return to Paris to obtain the assistance she needed. It would take time to plan, and plan she would; she now had a purpose for her anger and pain. She would drink to Pat's memory and the destruction of all that Larry White loved.

"*J*ustice is swift around here," Frank said.

Larry stood and looked into the trees. "Yes, it is."

"What's wrong?"

"These two are never far apart. Jam is out there and she probably watched this, which makes her even more dangerous," Larry told him.

"Get your men; we need to go. The Jedburghs will be arriving Monday and we are not even close to where they will be landing," Claud said.

Frank whistled for his men. Don and Robert gathered their belongings and joined the others.

"Did you hear or see anything?" Larry asked as they rejoined the others.

"Nothing," Don said.

The Americans and their friends disappeared into the night. Larry turned and looked into the trees as a chill ran down his back. "I know you're there."

CHAPTER THIRTY-FIVE

0030, Monday, December 13, 1943

*D*ealer was standing with the other Jedburghs, receiving final instructions, which included code words and the correct response. She could see the general standing at the back of the room. He had taken a huge chance sending her on this mission. She would make him and her country proud.

"That's all. Good luck, men and lass," the British officer said.

The man who had insulted her mother turned and said, "Move on, time to go."

"Sergeant McKenzie, I want to apologize," Dealer said.

"No need, lass, it was a test. You did jolly good. I am pleased to have you go with us."

Dealer followed the sergeant and General Fines to the plane. She turned and heard music—a song she knew, "Stormy Weather."

"What's wrong?" David asked.

"I hope that song is not an indicator of our trip," Dealer told him.

0300
France

"*D*amn, it's cold," Robert said.

"I don't envy those soldiers; the jump will not be pleasant," Larry said.

"They are very brave to do this so close to the enemy," Claud responded. "We must hurry to get them once they leave the plane. We are not the only ones out here."

"Frank, you're going to wear the image off the paper," Don teased.

"Ah, amour," Claud smiled. "She is your wife, yes?"

"Not yet, but one day. I miss her letters," Frank said.

"There will be a stack to read when we get back," Don laughed.

"I'm worried they have declared us all dead," Frank sighed.

"Probably just missing," Larry told him. "My family is probably worried too, but I have to see this through. Frank, anytime you want I will get you back."

Frank looked at his men. "We'll give it more time. I feel we are making some difference."

"You are, my friend," Claud responded.

"Listen, I hear something," Robert said.

"Time to go," Claud said.

*T*he door to the plane opened and the first blast of freezing air hit everyone.

"Up," Sergeant McKenzie said.

Dealer stood and checked her equipment once more. She could feel her legs shaking but told herself it was from the cold.

"Tuck and roll," David told her.

Dealer nodded her head. "I won't forget."

"See you in a few months," David smiled and watched as his Mississippi sprite walked to the door and jumped with the rest of the men.

"Godspeed."

"*F*rank, how many do you see?" Claud asked.

"Three, four, five . . . six total. The last guy is small," Frank answered.

The Maquis moved quickly to find the men who were landing in enemy territory.

"Where are they?" Larry asked.

"There, I see four," Don said.

The four men, led by Sergeant McKenzie, gave the code word and were relieved when the proper response was given.

"Jolly good, we need to find the other two."

At that moment gunfire was heard to their left.

"Go," Claud said, and everyone moved toward the sound of death.

*D*ealer was holding pressure on the wounded shoulder of her comrade.

"Harry, stay down," Dealer said. She heard more gunfire and someone yelling in French that help was coming. There were footsteps close and she heard someone ask for the code word.

"Bird in the hand," Dealer said.

"Many in the bush," the response was made.

"Here," Dealer called out.

"My name is Claud."

"Dealer."

"A woman?"

"Yes, can we go? He needs help," Dealer said.

Claud helped the wounded Jedburgh up and they moved away with cover fire from other Maquis.

Dealer was covering their retreat when she saw a German soldier about to shoot one of the Maquis. She pulled her weapon and dropped the enemy where he stood. When the Maquis turned to thank her she could not believe who she had just saved.

"Thanks, you shoot well for a little guy," Frank said, and waved to the soldier who had just saved him. "Drink later."

Frank didn't recognize me, Dealer thought.

"We must leave now," Claud said.

The Maquis disappeared with the Jedburgh and information that would be needed for the months ahead. Dealer stayed with her company and would wait for the appropriate time to talk to Frank. She watched as the Maquis, both men and women, splintered off into groups of three and disappeared. They were taken to a secluded farmhouse where Harry could finally receive medical attention. Dealer followed Claud, Frank, and someone called Larry inside with the others. Several men were left outside—some Maquis, others Americans.

"Sergeant, my people will take care of your man," Claud said.

"Happy to know that," McKenzie said. "We didn't plan to get so bloody close to Jerry."

"Sergeant, which one of your men saved my ass back there?" Frank asked as he grabbed a bottle of wine and opened it.

"Speak up. Who saved the yank?"

"I did," Dealer said, and walked around, took off her cap, and ran a hand through her mop of red hair.

Frank pushed everyone aside and grabbed, hugged, and kissed her in front of everyone.

"Amour, yes?" Claud said.

CHAPTER THIRTY-SIX

Saturday, January 29, 1944
Gloucestershire, England
Tortworth Castle

*S*usan sat on her cot looking at the picture of Angie, Jerry, and Junior. A tear slid down her face when she saw the flat sleeve pinned against his shirt. Angie's letter said Jerry was adjusting and the army promised prosthesis to help with his recovery. He was lucky when so many had died in the South Pacific. Eugene was listed as missing, possibly a prisoner of war. Jerry still planned to become a teacher and would start college this summer. There was a chance Jerry might get help from the government to pay for his college if something called the G. I. Bill was passed by the government. There had been no news from Bill for about two months but the army had not notified them either. They had received a letter informing the family Frank had been shot down and was missing, no other information. Angie said they would not give up hope, that Frank was strong and smart and would find his way home. The end of the letter said they were working on a sister for Junior. Susan smiled.

"What are you smiling about?" Nancy asked.

"Looks like I will be an aunt again by the time the war is over," Susan answered.

"Where are Dawn and Pam? Wait, don't tell me, another camp breakdown to the brass I saw arriving this morning?"

"Afraid so. I need to get busy and put my papers together for Lieutenant Fields. We have a new group coming in two weeks for surgical techniques and sterilization of instruments in the field."

"Prepare, share, rest, and recuperate—isn't that what they told us when we landed? I thought we were going to have some downtime to relax," Nancy sighed.

"What, the costume ball last weekend doesn't count?" Susan teased.

"You know what I mean; real time that we can go walk, eat cake, and drink tea like before," Nancy said.

"Let me see if the four of us can get a Jeep and take a ride in the country, have a picnic. We'll take B.O. for protection," Susan said, then started laughing.

Dawn and Pam walked into their room to the sound of hysterical laughing.

"Okay, this must be good. What did we miss?" Dawn asked.

"Oh nothing, just Susan suggesting we take B.O. as our protector on a picnic," Nancy said.

The laughter became louder as two more joined in. There was a knock on their door and all four stopped for a moment.

"It must be a damn good joke; care to tell me?" B.O. said.

The "Georgia Peaches" all broke out again in hysterical laughter.

"Ah, come on, tell me. I love a good joke."

Midnight
Gestapo Office
Paris

*J*am stood on the balcony and finished her cigarette. She had not bothered to cover herself and enjoyed the smiles of the soldiers below staring at her naked body, knowing their commandant was enjoying himself. Both men rubbed themselves when she touched her breast before going back inside. Jam turned on the bathroom light and looked in the mirror at the wavy blonde hair that hung on her shoulders. It was different and she had trouble adjusting at first, but the style suited her purpose. She had spent the last month preparing her revenge. Hans had been more than generous with her requests and it only cost what she enjoyed giving away. He was a simple man in bed with little experience, but eager to learn and never refused her advances. She now had an American passport and papers that said she was a nurse. In a few more weeks Jam would blend with other American nurses going to England. She had used the small amount of information about medical personnel at Gloucestershire to build on the possibility that there would be plans and important information needed for their cause. *If I can find Susan and her friends they will have this information,* Jam had told Hans. She would take and destroy what Larry desired most. Jam heard movement coming from the bed.

"Come back to bed. I have need of your body," Hans told her.

"You thirst for more? You could barely finish what you started," Jam teased.

"You are a bitch. But you are my bitch," Hans told her.

"For now," Jam said, and returned to his bed.

Farmhouse
France

Frank, Larry, and Claud sat together with Sergeant McKenzie and looked over plans and preparations for the American invasion of France.

"Our purpose here is to help the French resistance prepare," McKenzie said.

"Larry, I have been told that the other woman has returned to Paris and is living with the commandant. She has changed her appearance, cut and colored her hair to blonde, and she is going to some type of class. My people there are watching but unable to make any advance," Claud said.

"Can you find out what type of classes she is taking? It will help us to know and pass on that information to our people when we return. It sounds like she is preparing for some type of covert mission for the Reich. I think it is time we return to the land of the living," Larry said.

"Frank, if you and your men could wait a couple of weeks we have one last raid that needs your assistance. I will get the information you need," Claud inquired.

Frank stood. "That will be fine. Claud, can you come with me for a moment?"

When the door closed McKenzie looked at Larry. "I hope he isn't planning to steal one of my troops."

CHAPTER THIRTY-SEVEN

0700, February 14, 1944
Village Where Maquis Are Hidden

Frank walked toward the planning room where he knew Deelyn would be preparing to leave with the Jedburgh's this morning. The raids he and his men had agreed to make with the Maquis had been successful. It was now time for them to leave and rejoin the fight where they all belonged, in the air. Frank had one last thing to do before he left.

"Deelyn, we are about to leave. Can you walk with me for a moment?" Frank asked.

"Frank, I don't know. Sergeant McKenzie's orders are strict. We are to report at 0900," Dealer responded.

"You will be back by then. This is important to me," Frank said, and held out his hand.

"Okay."

Frank led Dealer quietly down the back streets and slipped into a small church where they sat down.

"Do you remember our meeting in the B-17?" Frank asked.

"How could I forget?" Dealer said and laughed.

"At that moment I thought you were something special, but when you walked into the officers' club that night, I fell in love with you."

"I . . . " Dealer started and looked up to see a priest lighting candles. "Should we be here?"

"Let me finish. We both have jobs to do but I don't want to go through the war without you here in my heart. Before we are separated by our duty to our country, will you marry me? Here . . . now?" Frank asked.

"Right now?" Dealer asked.

"Yes, right now."

Dealer looked up and saw Claud and Larry standing with the priest. "Frank, what I am doing here is important to me, to my country, and to General Fines. He took a huge chance sending me here. You can't tell anyone," Dealer said.

"Our secret. I promise," Frank said.

"We have to have a real wedding after the war," Dealer said.

"Agreed."

In the light of flickering candles two figures stood in silence while the priest spoke French and Claud interpreted for Frank. Promises made without rings to bind, only signatures in a church ledger. When the simple ceremony had finished Frank kissed his bride, a kiss that would have to suffice until the end of the war.

Noon

Larry and Frank gathered their belongings and information to take back to the allies. Frank had been quiet since their return from the church and the Jedburghs had left the house.

"She will be all right," Larry said.

"I guess so. She jumped out of a plane into occupied German territory, killed the enemy, and can fly a plane better than most pilots," Frank said.

"Hell of a honeymoon," Larry said and laughed.

Both men looked up as Don opened the door.

"Captain, you and Larry need to come out here," Don said.

"I think Claud has information about that other woman," Robert told them.

"My friends, I have news. The woman Jacqueline, or Jam, has been studying medical information. I am told she has an American passport and papers that say she is a nurse."

Larry's hands were shaking. "Where, where is she going?"

"To England. She left Paris today."

CHAPTER THIRTY-EIGHT

March 25, 1944
England

Susan was on her way back to Lieutenant Fields' office when she saw B.O. and her friends running toward her. Her heart began to beat rapidly and she prayed that what they had to say was not bad news.

"Susan! Susan, stop! Stop!" B.O. was yelling.

"Stop yelling! You're going to make her have a heart attack," Nancy told him.

Susan sat down on the ground; she was afraid she would faint.

"Honey, get up. You are going to dance a jig," Dawn told her.

"Go on, B.O., tell her," Pam said.

"They're alive. Larry, your brother Frank, and some of his men. They have been in France helping the Maquis."

Susan took a deep breath and smiled. "Where are they?"

"Your brother and his men are on their way to one of our bases here in England for debriefing and reassignment."

"And Larry?"

"Susan, he's on his way here," Nancy told her.

"Honey, he'll be here in a couple of days," Pam said.

Susan stood up and hugged B.O.

"Time to celebrate," Nancy said.

The "Georgia Peaches" continued with their celebration of good news when a group of nurses passed by and several of them stopped to see what the laughter was about.

"Good news?" the tall blonde asked and pushed her glasses up.

"Only the best," Pam said.

"You're the newest group to come in, aren't you?" Dawn asked.

"Yes, my name is Alice Jones, from Oklahoma," she said, and held out her hand to shake Dawn's. "What's the good news?"

"Susan's fellow is coming to see her," B.O. said.

"That's wonderful. When will he be arriving?" Alice asked.

"A couple of days," B.O. answered.

"Well congratulations. We need to run," Alice said, and left with her friends.

"B.O., you talk too much," Nancy said.

"What? They were just interested in someone's happiness," he responded.

"She looks familiar," Nancy said.

"What? You seeing spies again?" Dawn asked.

*A*lice returned with the others to their quarters. She walked into the latrine and looked in the mirror at the homely blonde reflecting back. Jam had made it. They didn't recognize her, but the smaller one, Nancy; she would have to kill her, too. Jam would have to move her plans up. Larry was returning quicker than she had expected. She would go back outside again tonight and find the location she would take Susan. She would leave a note for Larry in French, pinned to the little one. She would celebrate but there was no way to get a good bottle of wine here in this shithole. Jam could not wait to finish this, go back to Hans, and wait for the end of the war in luxury and comfort. She would bring good information, valuable information that would gain her favor and reward.

"Alice, time to go eat," one of the women in her group called.

Shit, bad coffee, bad food. "I'm on my way," Jam said. *For you, Pat, I'm doing all this for you.*

Allied Headquarters

*L*arry was trying to finish the last of his reports. He had been debriefed and flown to three different military headquarters to give the same report again and again. He could anticipate the next question and answer before it was asked. He had been permitted to call his family. His mother couldn't stop crying long enough to talk. Beatrice called him a name that was reserved for criminals, and his father said he had new gray hairs because of him. Emmitt said he was happy Larry was alive and hung up. Larry sent a telegram to Mr. Milton with the promise of a story to top anyone coming out of Europe. Frank said he would be proud to have him as his brother-in-law. They shook hands and Frank and his men left for home for some much needed R&R. Larry didn't think Frank would rest much worrying about his new bride traveling with the Maquis.

"Larry, you're needed. We have just a few more questions and then the doctors want to see you," the aide told him.

"Damn it! I have to be out of here tomorrow! Where's the general?" Larry asked.

CHAPTER THIRTY-NINE

0630, March 27, 1944
England

*J*am had everything ready. She now needed to slip away and separate the "Georgia Peaches" and finish this charade. Jam would not be in such a hurry to kill Susan. They needed some time to talk; she wanted Susan to know why this had been done. Jam wanted to see Larry suffer as she had when Pat died. Jam looked at the notes she had written to send everyone scattering across the compound—divide and conquer. She had her escape route set and arrangements for transportation back to Paris.

Alice looked in the mirror, adjusted her glasses, gathered her notes, and left her quarters for the last time.

"I'm not feeling well," Jam told the lieutenant.

"Infirmary is across the compound. Do you need to be driven?" Lieutenant Fields asked.

"No, I will make it."

"Someone will check on you later."

"Thank you," Jam said, and smiled as the lieutenant turned and walked away.

Jam quickly found two of Susan's friends and gave them notes, sending them to far corners of the compound to meet the lieutenant she had just talked with. The small one would not be so easy to fool.

0900

*N*ancy had been watching Alice from the window in their quarters. Something was not right. She had seen her give

Dawn and Pam notes. Alice should have been in camp breakdown and set-up this morning. The class had been suspended yesterday due to equipment failure. She needed to find the lieutenant and see why Alice was not where she should be. Nancy sat down on her bed and tried to think of where she had seen this Alice before. She took out the picture of Pat and Jam and found a pen. She drew glasses on Jam, and then shortened the hair. "It's her, the bitch is here," Nancy said out loud.

Nancy stood and started out the door. She had to find the lieutenant and Susan.

"Hello mon cher."

Nancy looked up and Jam knocked her to the floor.

*L*arry sat in the military transport, concerned about Susan and the others. The plane he was on was the fastest transportation, but with the stops to other bases to drop off supplies and men would cause a two-hour plane ride to become four. Jam could be there for several reasons but he felt Susan would be her main target. Any information she would gather for the Reich would be a cover for why she really came here. Larry looked up at the sergeant who walked toward him.

"We have contacted the base commander, sir. They are in the process of locking down and beginning the search."

"She will not be that easy to catch. I know; I chased her all over France, trust me," Larry told him.

1130

*S*usan had finished her work early and had been given the rest of day off and a two-day pass. She was on her way back to her quarters. She had not seen Dawn or Pam all morning and she wanted to talk to them before Larry arrived. B.O. was on his way to pick him up. He would be there at 1300, and then a short drive back and . . . Susan looked up as she entered her room.

"Come in, Susan, and join us. Your friend and I have been catching up," Jam said.

"Alice, what's going on, who are you?" Susan asked.

"I'm hurt, you don't remember me? My name is Jacqueline, or Jam," she said, and took her glasses off.

Susan realized this was the same woman in Ireland, the spy everyone was looking for. "What have you done to my friend?"

"Nothing that can't be corrected as long as you come with me," Jam told her.

Nancy was tied to her bed and gagged; her nose was bleeding. There were four small cuts, two on her wrists and two on her neck. They looked superficial but seemed to be bleeding more than they should. She looked at Jam, who was holding a small bottle.

"It's so interesting to know that this small bottle can help or kill. You should come with me, Susan, maybe your other friends will find her before she bleeds to death."

"Let me help her!" Susan screamed.

"I think not," Jam said, and pulled out a gun. "We need to go now. Larry took someone from me and now I will do the same."

Susan looked at her friend. "Lay still. Don't move. Try to slow your breathing."

"Good advice," Jam said, and pinned a note with Larry's name on Nancy's chest.

Susan looked back one last time; she could hear Judy's voice singing "The Old Rugged Cross." She prayed the others would find Nancy . . . and soon.

Noon

"*D*awn, what the hell is going on here?" Pam asked.

"I was going to ask you the same thing," Dawn answered.

"Where have you two been?" Lisa Fields asked both of them.

"We were given notes to meet you," both women told her.

"I didn't write these. Who gave these to you?" Lisa said.

"The blonde nurse from Oklahoma," Pam said.

"Alice something," Dawn said.

"She told me this morning she was ill and went to the infirm . . . Where are Nancy and Susan?"

"I guess they are in their quarters, why?" Dawn asked.

"Something is terribly wrong here. You two follow me, double time," Lisa said.

All three ran to the main quarters.

"Who locked the door?" Pam asked.

The sound on the radio had been turned up to its maximum volume. "I've Got a Gal in Kalamazoo," by Glenn Miller, was playing.

"Nancy, are you in there?" Lisa was screaming.

"Get out of my way," Dawn said, and kicked open the door.

"God in Heaven," Pam said.

"Go, Dawn, get help over here now," Lisa ordered.

Pam had already grabbed sheets and took the gag out of Nancy's mouth. "Nancy, honey, can you hear me?"

"She took her; that French bitch took Susan," Nancy finished and passed out.

Dawn returned, "Help is coming."

"What's this?" Pam asked, and held a bottle up for the lieutenant to look at.

"Christ, its Heparin," Lisa answered. "Look for more; we have to know how many were used."

"Two—this one and one more that is empty," Dawn said.

"Ladies, get over here, pressure until we can get her to the infirmary," Lisa said, and pulled the note from Nancy's blouse. "What's this? Who's Larry?"

"Larry White, someone Susan loves," Pam said.

"Nancy, stay with us, that's an order. Wake up, look at me," Lisa said.

1230

*L*arry got off the transport plane and could see B.O. "It's good to see you."

B.O. hugged him. "No, it's good to see you. Shit, you had all of us worried. We need to go. Susan is waiting for you."

"She's here, B.O," Larry said.

"Who's here?"

"Jam. She cut her hair, changed the color to blonde, wavy and has an American passport, may be wearing glasses to help with the disguise. Does that sound like anyone new in the camp?"

"Jesus Christ, we have to go now," B.O. told him. "Yes, I've seen her, talked to her; she knew you were coming today."

"Susan," Larry said.

As both men ran to the Jeep Larry could hear Frank Sinatra singing "I'll Never Smile Again" coming from one of the hangars.

1330

"*I* want that bitch found now," Lisa was yelling as Nancy was placed in the ambulance.

Dawn saw a Jeep pull up with Larry. "Pam, its B.O. and Larry."

Both women ran to the Jeep, followed closely by Lisa.

"What's happened?" B.O. asked.

"Jam, she almost killed Nancy. Gave her an overdose of Heparin and then cut her," Pam told them.

"Susan. Where's Susan?" Larry asked, already knowing the answer.

"The bitch took her," Lisa said to him. "This is for you but I want to know what the hell is going on before you open this."

"Long story short, German spy who watched her best friend executed and I was responsible for that death. Now she is going to take what matters most in my life from me . . . Susan," Larry said.

1400

Larry,

It will be nice to see you again. Most unfortunate we will not be able to share a bottle of French wine and sweet memories. I have something that is important to you. We must talk so you will understand why

Susan must die. Do not attempt to find me tonight; instructions will arrive tomorrow at noon; come alone.

Susan and I have much to talk about tonight, much to share. You understand.

Jacqueline

Larry read the letter out loud to everyone in the room.

"Bitch!" B.O. said.

"We'll find her," Pam said.

"No, this woman is not someone we can push. She will kill Susan and we'll never find her body," Lisa said. "This Jam has friends here and we don't have enough time to question everyone."

"We can't just sit here," Dawn said.

"Yes, we can, we have no other option at this moment," Larry said. "Where's Nancy?"

*N*ancy opened her eyes and saw everyone who was important to her at that moment. She looked at the tube that was delivering blood to replace what she had lost.

"Nancy, they have given you Protamine Sulfate to reverse the Heparin," Lisa said. "We found you in time."

"We're all here," Dawn said.

"Not all, Susan. She took her," Nancy said.

"Nancy, what did she say?" Larry asked.

"Susan came through the door and Jam told her you had taken someone from her and she was taking someone from you. Susan was so worried about me I don't think she heard her," Nancy answered.

"Did she say where they were going?" Pam interrupted.

"No, I'm sorry, I'm so sorry," Nancy said, and started to cry.

"That's enough. Everyone out of here," Lisa said.

"Nancy, I'll find Susan," Larry said.

1800
English countryside by the ocean

am watched as the man who brought food to the camp every day carried Susan into the abandoned shell of a house. It was so easy to get what you wanted with money. She had made a few improvements since they would be there overnight waiting for Larry. A mat, lantern, water, rations, and a few blankets. She would have to be careful of a fire though. *As long as I have wine I'll be good.* She watched as Susan was staked, no chance for her to escape.

"Anything else?" the man asked.

"Yes, you need to deliver this," Jam handed him a note with Larry's name on it. "Leave it in the mess tent, by the coffee."

"This will cost extra," he said.

"I fully expected it to," Jam said, walked up to him, dropped to her knees, and fulfilled the price of delivery.

usan opened her eyes and tried to adjust to the darkness that surrounded her. She had a headache from the sedative and was cold. Susan remembered the sight of Nancy and then leaving with Jam, but nothing as she exited the building. She tried to move but couldn't. She was basically staked down.

"I was beginning to think I gave you too much," Jam said.

Susan could see Jam by a small fire, drinking from a bottle. "Why are you doing this?"

Jam stood, walked over, slapped Susan's face, and then kicked her. "Because, you whore, Larry had my friend Pat killed in France. Tomorrow when he comes to save you I will kill you in front of him so he will know the pain of losing someone special."

Susan could feel blood oozing from her lip. "I have done nothing to you."

"You have been in my way since I first met Larry!" Jam was screaming. "I wanted him, offered myself to him, and all he could

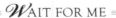

see was you. So I will remove you from his life, deny him a future of love and family."

Susan watched as Jam filled a syringe and walked over to her.

"Sweet dreams of death," Jam said, and stuck Susan in the shoulder.

Susan drifted off with the memory of holding her mother as she died in her arms.

CHAPTER FORTY

$\mathcal{L}$ arry sat in the office of Lieutenant Fields trying to answer the rest of her questions, waiting for the instructions Jam had promised. They both could hear B.O. coming down the hallway calling Larry's name.

"Damn it, man, this was left in the mess tent," B.O. said, and handed Larry the paper.

"From her?" Lisa asked.

"Yes," B.O. answered.

"How the hell is she getting things delivered on this compound? This means things are not secure," Lisa said, and picked up the phone to make a call.

"It's the directions and the same warning to come alone," Larry answered.

"Then I think you should do as she asks. It may be the only way to get Susan back alive," Lisa told him.

"Jam does not intend for Susan to live. I want medical units close if I should need them," Larry said.

"Larry, I don't like any of this," B.O. said.

Larry stood and walked to the window. "I do not have a good feeling."

1400

$\mathcal{J}$ am stood outside and checked her escape route one last time. This would have to all work together for her to get away. She walked back to the building and slapped Susan across the face.

"Wake up, slut, time to go," Jam said, and threw water in Susan's face.

Susan stood and Jam released the ropes. Susan turned, kicked Jam in the stomach, scratched her across the face, and ran out into the bright sunlight.

"I'm going to kill you!" Jam screamed.

Susan tried to get a quick view of where she could go. *Too much open ground, nowhere to hide.* She could hear Jam cursing and something she didn't expect—gunfire and a familiar voice . . . Larry.

"Susan, get down!" Larry yelled. "Behind you!"

Susan turned and faced Jam.

"Die whore, die," Jam said, then stabbed Susan and ran toward the cliffs.

Larry could not get a clear shot without hitting Susan. He watched as Jam shoved a knife into the woman he loved.

"No!" Larry ran and fired toward Jam, hoping one of his shots would kill her. He reached where Susan lay. He pulled the talkie out and called for medical assistance.

Larry fell to the ground and picked Susan up into his arms. He looked down into her face. "Susan, look at me! Don't leave, please don't leave me." At that moment Susan's face changed, changed into the face of the woman who had saved him at Pearl Harbor. The woman he now held was dressed in the same blue checkered dress stained with blood. She opened her eyes, reached up, and put her hand over the pocket that held the heart necklace and smiled.

"I found you once and you will find me again," she said.

Larry didn't understand but watched as she faded away. "Susan, Susan."

Susan opened her eyes. "I'll be waiting for you."

Larry held Susan to his heart. He could hear the sound of help coming, help that would be too late.

Infirmary

Nancy looked out the window. Clouds had gathered and it had begun to rain. There had been no word since Larry had left; no one had come to tell her Susan was okay. Nancy heard footsteps; slow, methodical thunder and lightning announced their arrival.

Lieutenant Fields, Dawn, Pam, and B.O. entered the room. There were no smiles, no joyful announcement that Susan had been saved. Red, swollen eyes and tears running down faces were all Nancy needed to see to know her friend would not be returning.

Larry started down the hallway to check on Nancy and the others when he realized he hadn't changed clothes. *I can't go in there like this,* he thought, and leaned against the wall outside the door.

"Larry, where have you been?" B.O. asked

"In the office sending word back to the Maquis. They have to stop Jam. She knows too much about the invasion of France," Larry answered.

"Do you think they will stop her?"

"I have faith in someone there. If anyone can find her the Jedburgh and the Maquis will and make sure she never tells anyone about D-day," Larry said. He looked at the blood that had dried on his clothes. "I have to go change."

"Will you be back? Nancy and the others want to see you."

"In a while. I need to be alone right now," Larry said, and walked away.

CHAPTER FORTY-ONE

1400, April 2, 1944
England

*L*arry sat alone in the chapel with the flag-draped coffin that held Susan's body. Tomorrow she would be flown back to the states, to her family. He took the necklace out of his pocket and held it in his hand, and as he expected the room filled with the scent of lilacs. *I found you once and you will find me again.* He didn't understand, he probably never would, but everything was connected to the heart he held in his hand. Larry knew he should have placed it in the coffin but he couldn't; it made him feel as if Susan was still there with him. No, he would keep it and pass it down as his grandfather had done. It was important; it would always be special. The doors to the chapel opened and people came until there was no more room. Susan had been liked, loved by many people, more than she realized. He felt a hand on his shoulder.

"Mr. White, we're ready to begin," the pastor said.

Larry stood, placed the necklace in his pocket closest to his heart, walked to the podium, looked out at the crowd, and began, "My name is Larry White and I have a story to tell you about a very special lady . . . "

France

"*D*ealer, I have information," Claud said.

"And a photograph?" Dealer asked.

"Yes, and a date when she will be arriving. How do you feel about a trip to Paris?"

Dealer turned and looked at Sergeant McKenzie. "Jolly good. We'll be here when you get back."

"Do I get to wear a dress?"

Claud smiled and the two of them disappeared.

Henry and Ida's home
Waynesboro

Henry sat in the main room of the house looking at the telegram that told when Susan's body would be arriving in Augusta. He, Jerry, and the boys would go to receive the coffin. Henry had warned her, told her there was danger, but she went anyway. He just never figured she would be murdered by a Nazi spy.

"Henry, Dr. Small is here. He says he has information," Ida said, her eyes swollen from crying.

"Henry, I am so sorry to hear about Susan. She and my daughter were very close. That is why I am here. Nancy is being sent home, discharged. The same spy who killed Susan almost killed my daughter," Dr. Small said.

"Oh my God, no," Ida said.

"She will be on the train with Susan's body and would like to stay here. Will that be okay with you?"

"You have been wonderful since Bill has been gone. There will always be room for you and your family here," Henry said, and looked up when Angie came into the room.

"Mom, where are the boys?" Angie asked

"Angie, what are you doing out of bed?" Dr. Small asked. "You need to be resting. This pregnancy is not like your first."

"I'll take her," Ida said, and headed Angie back to bed.

Henry looked at Dr. Small. "The boys and Jerry are at the family plot."

"Any word on Eugene?"

"Yes, his body arrives the day before Susan's," Henry said.

Dr. Small shook his head. "I am afraid there will be more to come before this war is over."

"I think you're right, Doc."

CHAPTER FORTY-TWO

1900, April 7, 1944
Paris

The car that waited at the airport for Jam had been obtained the night before. The blood had to be cleaned from the seats and uniforms repaired. Claud and Dealer now stood watching the plane land. The tall blonde walked down the stairs and waved at them.

"That's her," Dealer said.

"Time to finish what Larry started," Claud said. "Go. I will bring the car."

Dealer straightened the German uniform and walked up to Jam.

"Dame Jacqueline?" Dealer asked in French.

"Oui," Jam answered.

"Hans sent us."

"Bastard said he would be here himself," Jam said.

"He was delayed, matters of our Fuhrer," Dealer said, and opened the back door of the car.

"No matter, you will do," Jam said.

"Oui, I will," Dealer said, then took out the boning knife and entered the back seat with Jam.

Jam's body was left on the street in front of the Gestapo office in Paris, her throat cut with a message pinned to her chest: Death to all who betray their people. The information she carried died with her.

2200
New York

*N*ancy looked out the window of the train as it started again from the last stop. It had been hard to leave her friends, but the damage was done and she would never be at full capacity. Dawn and Pam would find her when they were discharged. Lieutenant Fields gave her personal information so she could keep in touch. Larry and B.O. were there with her when they loaded Susan's body on the plane. She remembered the look on Larry's face, his soul lost. Both men had been given options to return to the states if they wanted but decided to stay and finish the stories there in Europe, write about the war, the wins, and terrible losses. Nancy laid her head back and tried to rest; it would be late Saturday evening before the train arrived in Augusta. She closed her eyes.

"Excuse me, is this seat taken?" the male voice asked.

Nancy opened her eyes to see Bill Benjamin in uniform asking permission to sit. She stood, threw her arms around him, and began to cry.

CHAPTER FORTY-THREE

2200, April 8, 1944
Augusta

$\mathcal{T}$he arrival of the train in Augusta was without cheers or fanfare. Bill had sat and listened to the story of Susan and the "Georgia Peaches." She told him of their accomplishments and the story of the spy that took Susan's life. When Nancy reached for her bags Bill took them instead. He watched as Nancy got off the train and was embraced by her father and mother. When he stepped off he heard a familiar and welcomed voice.

"Son of a gun, Bill," Henry called, walked up, and hugged him. "Good God, you're skinny as a rail, son."

"It's good to see you, too; I just wished it was for another reason than this," Bill said.

"You know?"

"Nancy told me about Susan and that you almost lost Frank. I can't believe she's gone," Bill said, and wished he could cry, but the war had hardened a part of his soul.

"Bill, it's good to see you. Thank God you're home," Dr. Small said, and shook his hand.

"Things have been rough. Jerry lost his arm, Eugene was killed—we buried him today—Angie's having problems with this pregnancy, Frank, Susan, it's more burden than any one family should have to carry," Henry said.

"Dad, we need you," Jacob said.

The men on the landing turned and saw the compartment door of the train open, which held Susan's body. Without further conversation they gathered and took charge of the coffin. Nancy stood sniffing with her mother's arms around her.

"You understand, don't you, Mother? I have to go with her. I'm family; we went through so much together, I . . . "

"Yes, baby, I understand. You can come home when you're ready," Mrs. Small said.

"Susan's body was placed in a hearse borrowed from the local funeral home in Waynesboro.

"Where are we taking her?" Bill asked Henry.

"Home."

0300, April 9, 1944
Waynesboro

"*I*da, I can go home," Bill insisted.

"Absolutely not, we have plenty of room, and besides, I need to get up there and open the house up, air things out. No one has been in there since you left," Ida responded. "Besides, it's nice to have you back home, you're too damn skinny and need to be looked after for a bit; no arguments."

Bill smiled. He knew better than to argue. "Okay, for a few days anyway."

"Henry, where is that young woman, Nancy?" Ida asked.

"I left her at the big house with Susan. She said she didn't want to leave her alone just yet," Henry answered.

"Bill, will you go and see if you can talk her into coming back? I don't like her color and the day has been hard," Ida requested.

"I'll do what I can," Bill said, and left for the big house. Bill's last memory of Susan was there in the big house. As he walked up the steps he could hear Nancy talking to Susan.

"I love your family, and Bill's home. He's too skinny. I think he has been sick but I'm not sure. I'm so sorry I wasn't strong enough to stop this, to save you . . . "

"Nancy, Ida wants you to come back. It's late," Bill told her.

"I can't leave her," Nancy said.

"I understand, believe me, but you're tired, I'm tired, and it will be a long day once the wake begins. We need to be at our best for her."

Nancy nodded her head. Bill watched Nancy walk to the coffin and place her hand on it. Bill and Nancy left the big house in silence, their sorrow shared with the night birds that called for morning to come.

2:00 p.m., April 10, 1944
Bowen Family Cemetery

The body of Susan would be laid to rest next to her aunt Sarah. Family and friends for miles had come to pay their respects. One by one those closest placed roses on the coffin and then watched it lowered into the earth. The mourners gathered back to the big house to eat and talk of the special person Susan had been, and for others their plans for the future.

"Bill, when do you have to go back?" Dr. Small asked.

"I'm not."

"You don't have to go back?" Nancy asked.

"No, discharged. Malaria almost killed me, so they sent me home," Bill said. "Nancy, I understand you have been discharged, too."

"Yes."

"I am going to need a nurse; would you be interested?" Bill asked.

"Yes, I would love to work for you and be near the people Susan loved."

"You can stay here until we can open another house," Ida said.

The conversation was interrupted by a knock on the door. Ida rose and opened the door. "Can I help you?" Ida looked at a man and woman dressed in uniform.

"My name is Judy Lowe and this is my fiancé, Isaiah. Susan was my friend and we are here to pay our respects."

"Come in, you are welcome in our home," Ida said.

CHAPTER FORTY-FOUR

December 15, 1944
Houston, Texas
Ellington Field

ealer was looking at the paperwork that ended her career as a WASP as of the twentieth of this month. She had been back only two months and had been through so much but couldn't tell anyone. She really was living a chapter of "The Shadow."

"Ready to go?" Thelma asked.

"Yes, called my folks and told them I would be home after the first."

"Then let's pack up and head to San Francisco for Christmas. One last flight thanks to your friend the general," Thelma said.

Dealer remembered him pinning the bronze and silver star on her and smiled when she received the Croix de Guerre. She was debriefed and reminded of the classified mission she had been on in France. She had signed papers stating she would keep secret all she had been involved with during her time with the Jedburghs.

"You're different since you've been back. I can't put my finger on it but you've changed," Thelma said.

"Really? I hadn't noticed," Dealer said and smiled.

Thelma put her arm around Dealer and they left to go pack up their apartment, ship their belongings home, and prepare for their last flight together as WASPs.

❦

December 24, 1944
Southern England
Base Command for B-17

"Don, let's go!" Frank said.

"Men are already on the plane," Don responded.

Robert stuck his head out the side door. "Damn, it's been nice to be back flying all these missions again." Then he let out a yell.

Frank slid into his seat, took Dealer's photo, and placed it where he could see it. "Gentlemen, we are about to make history."

Frank and his men were about to join the largest air strike of the war against Germany.

CHAPTER FORTY-FIVE

April 30, 1945
Dachua Concentration Camp

*L*arry and B.O. entered gates that had the German words "ABEIT MACHT FREI" at the top, but what they found had nothing to do with those words.

"Larry, what does that say?" B.O. asked.

Larry found one of the American soldiers who spoke German for the translation.

"It says: Work makes you free."

The two men looked at the prisoners, hundreds who were filthy, starved, sick, and dying. The stench of disease and death surrounded everyone. They were sprayed with DDT before being allowed to go further into the camp. Both men walked through the camp back to where they could see smoke.

"Oh, God," B.O. said, and vomited.

Larry stood unable to move. The sight of naked bodies stacked one upon another waiting to be burned had stunned him.

"I never thought I would say this but I'm glad Susan doesn't have to see this."

"The medical personnel will be here in a couple of days. Pam and Dawn will be among them," B.O. said.

"They'll hold up," Larry responded.

Larry turned away, thinking about all that he and B.O. had gone through since Susan had been murdered. The battles, the death of the president, and now this atrocity—it seemed there was no end.

"B.O., get your camera out. This has to be documented so no one ever forgets," Larry said.

Both men went to work, recording on film and paper all they had discovered. Eight days later, May eighth, Germany surrendered. Hitler, along with many of his men and their families, committed suicide.

✦

May 9, 1945
England

$\mathcal{F}$rank sat with the other captains, all of whom opened their packets, which explained their next assignments. The meeting lasted for about an hour. The information he had in his hand was not what he had expected and now he must tell his men their hopes of home would have to wait.

"You men have all the information you need. Good luck and Godspeed. Dismissed," the colonel said.

Frank walked back to his plane where his men seemed to be celebrating with others.

"Captain, when are we going home?" Robert asked.

"I bet the first thing you're going to do is find that redhead, right?" Don teased.

Frank stopped and looked at his men. *This is not going to be easy to say*, he thought. "Men, we're not finished. Home will have to wait."

The smiles and laughing ceased.

"Where are we going?" Don asked.

"Okinawa."

"For how long?" Robert asked.

"Until we win," Frank answered.

✦

June 1, 1945
Allied Air Base
Munich

"$\mathcal{A}$re you sure you won't stay? There's still so much to document and report," B.O. asked.

"I've seen enough, lost . . . "

"Where are you going? New York?"

"No, home to Hawaii. I need to get busy and tell what has happened here," Larry said. "What about you? We could use another good reporter in Honolulu."

"Think I will hang around for little while longer. Maybe settle down in Macon."

Larry laughed. "Congratulations, you and Pam make quite a pair."

"Yeah, she's a sweetie. Things just kind of happened," B.O. said and smiled. "Have you thought about going to Waynesboro?"

"I've thought about it but don't think it's a place I need to go right now. I'm not ready," Larry said.

"Well, look me up in Macon someday, would you?" B.O. asked.

"I'll do that," Larry said and held out his hand.

"Oh, you're not gonna get by that easy," B.O. said, and grabbed Larry and hugged him. "Take care."

"You, too."

CHAPTER FORTY-SIX

January 14, 1946
Leland, Mississippi
Johns' Hangar

ealer was working on the Waco trying to make it last one more year. She heard her paw's truck drive up to the hangar. She could hear his footsteps. She hoped he had a letter from Frank.

"Paw, I don't know if I can fix it this time. We need new parts," Dealer said.

"Maybe you can find what you need in Texas," a familiar voice answered.

"Frank!" Dealer screamed, bumped her head, and then jumped off the plane.

Frank held and kissed his wife, then wiped the grease off the end of her nose. "I've got sixty days. Is that enough time for a wedding?"

"Yep, I think so."

Butch had been standing back watching the scene unfold before him. He took a red work rag out and blew his nose.

"You got a good man there, Deelyn."

"I know, Paw, I know," Dealer answered.

Waynesboro, Georgia
Dr. Benjamin's office

ancy, can you go see who just came in? I don't remember anymore appointments today," Bill asked.

Nancy walked to the front of the office. "No, it can't be."

Bill heard Nancy scream and ran to the front to see her hugging two women who stood in uniform, with a man standing away from the three.

"It's so good to see you," Nancy said, tears falling down her face.

Dawn and Pam stood back to look at their very pregnant friend.

Nancy started to laugh. "Ladies, B.O., this is my husband Bill, Bill Benjamin."

"Nancy, we've come . . . " Dawn began.

"I'll take you; can all of you stay for a while?" Nancy asked.

"I think we can spare a few days and catch up on all the news," Pam said.

"B.O., it's good to see you, too. What . . . ?" Nancy started when she looked at the ring on Pam's finger. "No, when?"

"New Year's Day," B.O. said. "I have a job in Macon waiting."

"Dawn is going career," Pam said.

"Bill, can you close up? I'm going to take our friends home," Nancy said.

Bill walked over and kissed his wife. "I'll be along shortly."

"Nancy, can we go see Susan?" Dawn asked.

"She would like that, all of us here together again," Nancy said.

Nancy and her friends took the short ride to the family plot where final respects were paid to their friend. They stood and remembered all they had shared together, life and death in another part of the world. The "Georgia Peaches" were together again.

CHAPTER FORTY-SEVEN

February 17, 1946
Waynesboro, Georgia
The Big House

The Bowen family had pulled together as they always did, to make Frank and his new wife feel welcome. The big house once again knew laughter and happiness. The reception held no boundaries for food, music, and drinks.

"Frank, you have so much family," Dealer said.

Frank started laughing. "No more than yours."

So much had happened since Frank and Dealer had been remarried on Valentine's Day in Leland. Neither had taken the time to adjust to all the celebrating and all the family they now had together. Frank had not heard about Susan's death until he read Ida's letter upon returning to Texas after the surrender of Japan.

"How much time do you two have left?" Jerry asked.

"I have to report back to Randolph on the eighteenth of March," Frank said.

"I heard Deelyn say you made Major."

"Yes, promoted just before I left to find Deelyn, helped get me an extra thirty days."

"Mrs. Bowen . . . " Dealer started

"Aunt Ida or Ida, Deelyn, we're family now."

"Ida, I have a question about the names at the cemetery," Dealer said.

"Which ones?"

"Martha, Ethan, and Sarah, but what I really want to know first is Martha's maiden name," Dealer said.

Frank and Henry heard the question and walked up to the conversation.

"Why do you want to know?" Henry asked.

"My grandpa was born and raised in Louisiana, fought with the South. During the war a group of brothers came to my grandpa's home to join the fight around New Orleans. They said they were our kin. Grandpa always swore we didn't have any kin in Mississippi but his paw read the letter from their maw and took them in. These boys told him about their sister, a spitfire of a girl who had run off to deliver a letter and then planned to join the South and fight as a man. She was small of stature, often mistaken for a boy. Her hair was black as the night and cut short."

Henry and Frank looked at each other, and then at Ida. Angie and Jerry had walked up to listen to the rest of this story.

"The letter Mack ran off to deliver was from a boy named Ethan to his sister Sarah," Dealer said.

"Aunt Sarah's journal, Susan took it with her," Angie said.

"It wasn't in her belongings the military returned," Henry said.

"Maybe Nancy will know where it is. She and Bill have already left. I'll go call," Angie said.

"Henry, go get the family Bible," Ida said.

"Deelyn, what was her name?" Angie asked.

"Well Grandpa said her brothers called her Mack, but her full Christian name was Martha Ann Catherine Keens. My grandpa was Ernest Keens."

Ida took the Bible and looked at the family tree. "Frank, your grandmother's last name was Keens, Martha Ann Catherine Keens."

"Well this is interesting," Frank said.

"Does this mean we can't be married?" Dealer asked.

Everyone laughed.

"Did your grandfather ever say what was in the letter the boys had brought with them?" Jerry asked.

"No."

Angie returned after making the call to Nancy. "She said that Susan mailed it back to the states, she thought she mailed it here."

"It's probably lost," Henry said.

"This is unbelievable," Ida said. "Deelyn, just because your grandfather had the same last name doesn't mean you were truly related. It sounded like he had some doubt."

"Ida, is there an Ernest Keens in there anywhere? I know Martha put the names of all her brothers in there. She might have put other family names there, too," Henry said.

"I don't see anyone listed here by the name of Ernest."

"I just can't believe the two of you found each other," Angie said.

Frank walked over, pulled Dealer to him, and kissed her. "Fate."

CHAPTER FORTY-EIGHT

March 28, 1946
Honolulu, Hawaii

*L*arry had settled back into the routine of work. Stories about the war in Germany, the surrender of Japan, and his series on the battlefield nurses had kept him busy since his return. He lit a cigarette and turned his chair toward the window. There was still work to be done. The beauty of the island soothed his soul and he never tired of the sunsets. He had returned to his morning swims and surfing on the weekends, anything to keep him busy.

"Larry, what are you still doing here?" Mr. Milton asked. "I'm glad to have you back but you seem to be overdoing it."

"I need the distraction."

"Did I hear your family is coming?" Mr. Milton asked.

"Yes, but not for another month."

"I expect you to take off while they are here, and that is an order."

Larry smiled. "I think I might do that and work on my book."

"You amaze me; now go home. Oh, I almost forgot, this came for you today. It was mixed up in my mail," Mr. Milton said.

Larry took the package and saw it was from his brother. "Thanks." Larry stood, and both men walked over to the window and watched as the sun set.

Larry left the newspaper, stopped at the local liquor store, and bought a bottle of red wine. Once home he warmed leftovers in the oven, turned the radio on, and opened the wine. He sat on the balcony and ate his dinner. Larry returned for one more glass of wine and the package.

Two years ago today Susan had died in his arms. He went to his bedroom and found the necklace. Larry held it to his heart. *You will find me again.* He could still hear her; not Susan, but the woman who had appeared twice to him. Larry sat down, took the package, and removed the brown paper to see Susan's handwriting. He gently removed the second wrapping and found a book. He opened the cover to find a letter addressed to him.

Larry,

I sent this for safekeeping and will pick it up after our night out in New York. If you get back before I do, you might want to read this. Who knows? There might be a story here about our families . . .

Please wait for me. I long to hold you in my arms.

Love always,

Susan

Larry dropped his head and began to cry. The radio began to play "Til the end of time," by Perry Como. The scent of lilacs softly caressed him. Larry wiped the tears away, let his vision clear, opened the journal, and began to read about the argument between a brother and his sister.

EPILOGUE

arry took Sarah's heart and locked it away for the next forty-seven years. Her image was not seen on the battlefields that followed World War II, nor were there Whites or Shaws to report those wars. It seemed time had been frozen by Susan's death.

The years progressed and Larry never made his trip to Waynesboro. He did keep his promise to those who had meant so much to him during the war and spoke to them often by phone. When Frank retired from the military years later he and Dealer made San Antonio their home. Dealer continued to fly and did private charters. They had four children—three boys and one girl. Dawn became career military and was stationed for a short time in Hawaii. When she was promoted to lieutenant colonel, Larry wrote an article on her history and service to the country. Pam and B.O. had five children together and lived in Macon the rest of their lives.

Larry was given the opportunity to go back and follow American troops to Korea, but he declined. He remained busy at the newspaper and completed three books. Two of his accomplishments were about the war itself; the third was personal and unpublished. After he completed reading Sarah's journal and learned of a love that had not ended with death, Larry began the third book. It was about the lives of two families intertwined through bravery and chance, but there were still some parts missing, questions unanswered. Those questions could only be answered by the Bowen family.

The manuscript of this book was now boxed, along with personal items belonging to Sarah Bowen. This box would go to his great nephew—the one with aspirations of becoming a war correspondent, which made Larry smile. There was a letter to this new generation in the hope that he would understand all that Larry had survived and all that had been lost.

"Mr. White, your attorney is here," the nurse said to him.

"Send him in," Larry said.

"Yes, sir."

"*L*arry, you're looking good today," Bentwood Milton said.

"You're a horrible liar. I'm dying and I need you to do something once I'm gone," Larry said.

A young Bentwood Milton looked at this frail man who was his client and a dear friend. "Anything, Larry."

Larry pushed the package and an envelope toward Bentwood. "I want you to deliver this personally. There are instructions and a check for your fees."

"This must be special."

"It is," Larry said.

"Who and where?" Bentwood asked.

"Taylor Shaw, at the *White Daily Journal*," Larry said.

"New York?"

"Yes, New York," Larry answered.

"Larry, what is this?" Bentwood asked.

"My legacy."

FIND ME AGAIN

October 7, 2001

*J*ace stood at Cemetery Hill and looked over the battlefield. She had driven into Gettysburg around five, checked into a local hotel, grabbed a map and a bottle of water, and headed out for an evening walk. She would take the bus tour tomorrow and get a true feel for the battles that took place here. Jace chose to come in the fall, hoping the summer heat had subsided, as she loved the changing colors of the northeast. She took a deep breath of crisp air and felt the beginning of an October chill. She thought about the history, the great amount of death, and how nurses had worked with little or nothing to try to save the men and boys who were injured on the ground she now walked.

There were stories that had been handed down through her family about Sarah, an ancestor who was a nurse here at Gettysburg. Jace remembered the book written about Northern and Southern nurses who had traveled during the Civil War. She regretted not bringing it with her for reference, but felt it was safe in Galveston with her friends. This ancestor had actually traveled from Georgia with other nurses to heal. *Must be in our blood*, she thought.

Jace looked at the monuments that marked the leaders who were injured or killed along with troops from every part of the states that fought and died. She smiled at the locals who walked the grounds in costume, part of the charm of Gettysburg.

On her way back to the hotel she saw one of the locals in costume sitting on a bench. She walked up and smiled at the stranger.

"Mind if I sit down?" Jace asked.

"Please," the stranger said, and pointed to a place next to him.

"Nice evening," Jace began, and looked into the greenest eyes she had ever seen.

"Yes, so much nicer than the summers here," he said. "Are you staying long?"

"Couple of days . . . tourist," Jace answered, and turned to the sound of music that had started up the street.

"Be sure to go out to the Monfort farm," he said.

"Oh, really, why?" Jace asked, and turned back to an empty seat where the stranger had been sitting. She looked up and watched as he walked away from the town. The man stopped and turned around to look at her.

"There is a special story there, one you will want to hear," he said, and disappeared into the dark.

The next morning Jace decided to rent a bicycle and do the tour on her own. She put a few things in her backpack to get her through the day. Jace headed out to really listen and learn about what took place at Gettysburg those three days in July.

Jace passed characters who walked the streets and she smiled as soldiers tipped their caps, women curtseyed, and children played with toys that didn't require batteries. She looked for the man she had talked with the night before but didn't see him. Jace had hoped he would go with her since he seemed to have interesting information about this town and its history. She took the map and headed toward the first site.

As the day progressed Jace kept thinking about the Monfort farm and looked for its location on the map. She had one more day there before heading home to Galveston and decided to go on to the farm and finish the tour tomorrow.

As Jace rode up to the farm she could see a few cars and people walking around. She walked up, pulled out her camera, took a photo, and looked at the image. *That's funny, he wasn't there a minute ago,* she thought. The man she talked with last night was in her photo and now beckoned. "You found it," he said.

Jace walked up to this man dressed in the same clothing from the night before. "You said there is a story that I need to hear?"

"There were many important stories on all the battlefields here, but this one will touch you," he said. "Please sit down with me."

Both sat down in the grass and Jace listened to a story this stranger seemed to think would be of interest to her.

"There was a young nurse here who fell in love with a man who fought the war with a pen, not a weapon."

"A reporter," Jace said.

"Yes, these two were destined to be together, for they had known one another since childhood but had never met until the war. They found love in the midst of pain and suffering all around them. They became separated but he searched and was led to this farm, a hospital, to find and be with her forever. But fate can be cruel, and an unfortunate accident stopped their happiness. He died in her arms here at this place."

Jace wiped the tear away that ran down her face. "Such a sad story."

The stranger smiled. "But there is always hope where love is involved. The nurse promised to search for him for eternity until they were reunited. She had given him something very special . . . her heart."

Jace listened to this story and her own heart ached for these two lost souls. She then realized the day was rapidly ending and she needed to head back to town before dark. "Thank you for the story, but I need to go. I must apologize for not introducing myself last night. I'm Jace, Jace Bowen."

The stranger smiled again. "I'm Samuel, Samuel White."

ABOUT THE AUTHOR

Janet K. Shawgo has worked as a travel nurse for over sixteen years, specializing in high-risk labor and delivery. She has traveled across the United States, working in numerous hospitals. This is her second book in the "Look for Me" series. She again combines her passion for nursing with her interest in women's roles on the battlefields. She resides in Galveston, Texas.